MW00596485

THE
SHRIMP
DID
IT

SOUTHERN
BEACH
MYSTERIES

THE
SHRIMP
DID
IT

KAY DEW SHOSTAK

Kay Dew Shostak

THE SHRIMP DID IT
Copyright © 2020 by Kay Dew Shostak.
All rights reserved.

ISBN: 978-1-7350991-1-8

SOUTHERN FICTION: Cozy Mystery / Southern Mystery / Florida Mystery / Island Mystery / Empty Nest Mystery / Clean Mystery / Small Town Mystery

Text Layout and Cover Design by Roseanna White Designs
Cover Images from www.Shutterstock.com

Author photo by Susan Eason with www.EasonGallery.com

Published by August South Publishing. You may contact the publisher at:
AugustSouthPublisher@gmail.com

*Dedicated to the Amelia Island Shrimp
Festival committee,
especially my friend, and one of the festival
leaders, Pat Kaminski.
The joy with which they fulfill the
thousands of tasks necessary for the Shrimp
Festival to happen each year is evident
in every parade step taken and every
delicious shrimp enjoyed!
Make plans to join us next year—always
the first weekend in May!*

And as always,

*To our home –
Amelia Island and Fernandina Beach*

*While Sophia Island and Sophia Beach are
based on you,
the characters and situations can only be
found in my imagination.
Oh, and in my books.*

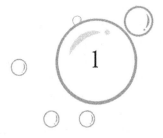

1

"'Told you I was sick'... that's what should be on her tombstone," Lucy Fellows says as she lays down her laminated, single-sheet menu. Our Wednesday lunches have moved to more remote restaurants as the popular eateries downtown and at the beach are filled with the beginnings of the summer crowds. We're actually off the island at a small bistro in a strip mall between a resale shop and a tanning salon. Who would've imagined they'd have tanning salons in Florida?

Lucy raises an eyebrow as she looks around the table and is met with shrugs, nods, and small smiles. Apparently everyone here but me knew the dearly departed and agrees with Lucy's assessment. But then, I *am* the new kid on the block, and I'm getting good at asking questions. If you don't, I've learned, my friends will go on like you've always lived here and know what they are talking about. "So, someone died?"

Next to me, Annie Bryant stops fanning herself with her menu and lets out a big sigh. "Yes, but no worries. Not like back in the spring when we seemed to fall over a dead body every time we turned around!"

"Very unseemly, Mrs. Mantelle, the way you came to town and kept finding murder victims," Charlotte Bellington says with a sniff. She's the oldest of the group and, I'm pretty sure, the meanest.

But she's right.

Craig and I moved to Sophia Beach, Florida, at the end of February, and the first time I went to lunch with this group, we mistook a dead body in the marina for a manatee. Then, only a few weeks later, I was the first to spot a young woman, also deceased, hidden in a fake turtle nest. It's a matter of pride in this group that a few of the members feel we solved both murders.

Lucy waves her hand toward the hostess stand. "I told them we wanted to order at noon. I can't lollygag here all day. With Memorial Day weekend just past and Amanda's funeral coming up, this week is jammed full.

I should've canceled lunch like I usually do after a holiday."

"Oh, is that why there's such a small group today?" I ask, but then the waitress sails to our table, so our ordering takes over the conversation.

There are usually a dozen or so ladies at our lunches. We get an email from Lucy each week telling us where we'll be eating, and we let her know if we will be coming. It's a great way to get to know people, and that's all it's for. No responsibilities, no causes, nothing but lunch and talk. Today there is only a handful of us, the detective ladies, which includes me; Annie Bryant, the vivacious mother to six adult children who all live on Sophia Island; Lucy Fellows, who runs this group and more committees than I can count; Tamela Stout, a recently retired teacher who's lived here almost two decades; and Cherry Berry, a part-time nurse who moved here only a couple of years ago with her husband. Charlotte Bellington is not officially part of our detecting group, but Tamela is her ride to lunch, so she's also here. There are two more ladies, but they are at the other end of the table, don't come very often, and seem content to chat with each other.

"There. Now that our orders are placed,"

Lucy says as she turns in her seat to face me, "we want to hear about your weekend."

Eager faces stare at me, and I see why we are having lunch during a busy, shortened week. But I guess this is just another part of having friends—something I'm trying to get used to. Tucking my hair behind my ears I sit up tall and lift my chin. "It went well. Everyone came. They had fun. Everyone left."

Tamela winks at me. "Everyone leaving. Sometimes that's the best part."

I smile tightly at her but can't think of what else to say. The huge, old house Craig inherited in the historic downtown area brought us here for retirement and a renewal of our marriage. Just the two of us. We left our four grown children back in the Midwest. Our twin daughters reside with their husbands in Chicago and St. Louis, one with a toddler and one with a baby on the way. Our two sons are students at the University of Wisconsin. All seven of them—six adults and our eighteen-month-old grandson—descended on our new North Florida adventure for Memorial Day weekend. Getting the creepy, dark, junky old house ready for them has been all I've thought about, and talked about, for the past month, so of course the ladies want a report.

But where do I start?

Cherry, ever the practical one, helps me out. "What did they think of the house?"

Except that apparently doesn't help, as tears spring to my eyes. With a tiny shake of my head, I blurt out, "The house was too hot. They weren't used to it. My daughter Sadie's husband couldn't sleep, and he got rooms at a hotel on the beach for him and her and Carver. I was so excited to have time with Carver at our house."

Annie, who kept her menu to fan herself with, fans even faster as she moans, "Oh man, I was worried about that with you having just two window units. Folks from up north just can't handle this humidity."

Charlotte smirks. "Maybe you shouldn't pass judgment as you blast the rest of us with your menu-powered wind tunnel."

Annie frowns at her. "I have an excuse. I'm a woman of a certain age, and these hot flashes are like to kill me." She shoots a deeper frown at Charlotte, but sympathy floods her face as she leans toward me and pats my arm. "Honey, don't let all that upset you. I'm sure that baby will remember being at your house more than that silly hotel."

"My house?" I surprise myself with my raised voice. "With a pool at the hotel? And the beach? They had their own little family vacation. We rarely saw them. Then poor Erin, she's the twin that's pregnant, she was sick most of the time and couldn't go far from the bathroom. That husband of hers just wanted to play golf all the time."

One of the ladies at the end pipes up. "We do have some fabulous golf courses, and if she was that sick…" She trails off as Annie widens her big, blue eyes and raises her eyebrows.

With a sniff, I have to agree. "I know. Erin really did want him to have a good time. And, all in all, I guess we did. My boys, Chris and Drew, loved it here. They took a surfing lesson, went out on jet skis, and both say they'll be back soon. So I guess that's good." Smiling around the table, I see that it's not enough. They want to know more. They want to know about—

"Craig? How were things with you and Craig?" Tamela asks. "He did come home, didn't he?"

Seeing the waitress coming our way with our food, I say quickly, "He picked up the boys from the airport Thursday night on his way in and dropped them off at the airport on his way back out of town Monday evening."

I study the waitress to avoid the looks of sympathy, anger, and frustration around the table. Any of those emotions would fit, as they are all still swirling in my head. I think my friends pick up on the fact that I'm not ready to talk about it because, after our food is placed in front of us and the waitress has left, Annie definitively changes the subject. "So, apparently Amanda Raines really was sick this time?"

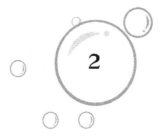

2

"Who wants to go over to the resale shop?" Annie asks as we step out of the dark restaurant and into the bright, hot parking lot. "I have a little time before I have to go take care of my grandkids."

Cherry nods and pauses on the sidewalk as Tamela shakes her head and rolls her eyes behind her passenger, Charlotte. The older woman walks past us, saying, "Paying good money for other people's junk is why this world is going broke. Tamela, it's time to go home."

Lucy is already in her car, with the air conditioner cranked up, typing on her phone. She's either headed back to work at the chamber of commerce or off to one of her myriad meetings—I can't keep her schedule straight. Lucy is single and dates one of the owners of the Sea Island Resort. She lives with her mother in the family beach house and runs most of Sophia Island from what I can tell. She's petite, blonde, and an avid tennis player, so nothing like me on several fronts. We left the other two ladies at the table, working out plans for a church function they are chairing.

I peel off toward my car, but Annie grabs my arm. "Come on. You don't need to go back to that house yet. Stay and play with us!" She laughs and drags me toward the shop's door.

We file inside and leave off talking as we each find things to look at. I've purposely headed away from the furniture. Our house came jam-packed full of old furniture, very little of it worth anything. Annie's son's girl-friend, Eden, helped me sift through what was good and what I should donate. I'm willing to bet some of the small tables and old chairs here came from my house, so I've seen enough old furniture to last a lifetime. I pull some scarfs from a pile and hold them up to look at their length. I love scarfs, but being tall, I always have to make sure they're long enough to not look silly on me.

Annie comes up to my elbow and sighs.

"Those are pretty. No new books, so I'm ready to go. Where's Cherry?"

"Over in the dishes. So, you're keeping the grandkids today? How are Amber and Mark doing?"

"Not those grandkids. Didn't I tell you? Amber and Mark moved lock, stock, and barrel out to his farm when school let out." Annie's heavyset and as tall as I am. Her bracelets rattle as she lifts her arms to lean on one of the circular clothing racks. "I have to admit I miss Leah and Markie, and even their dog, Oscar. I got used to them all being around so much, but I do hope their parents can make things work this time. Honestly, a humbled Amber is not a bad thing for the marriage. She's lucky to have gotten out as easy as she did from all that stuff up in The Settlement."

"So, she didn't lose her real estate license or anything?"

The dead young woman we'd found in the sea turtle's nest had been renting a space illegally in one of the old homes Amber owns, and with her death, all of Annie's daughter's dealings had come under a microscope with not only the real estate licensing board but also the IRS. Much as her siblings had been warning her would happen at some point.

Annie raises her eyebrows at me. "Nope. She shut down all of her off-the-books rental properties, paid some fines, and donated a piece of land for a little park up there."

"A park? I still haven't been up there. What is The Settlement exactly?"

"Where the town was originally, up on a bluff—well, as much of a bluff as you can have in Florida. It's where the original fort— Spanish, I believe—was. You can see way up the river, and there are old houses there that are being refurbished. Sunsets are wonderful from up there, and there's a bench to sit on. You remember that movie *Pippi Longstocking*? It was filmed here, and the house is still up there. Looks just like in the movie."

"No way! My girls loved that movie."

"Yep. Folks are pretty proud of living up there, but several had done what Amber was doing. They were renting out rooms without permission, so I think that's why everything just went away with no problems for her. Plus, some folks are trying to change the laws for long-term rentals, so no one wanted to make a fuss. While it was scary for her, it all ended okay. And like I said, a humbled Amber is a good thing." Annie straightens up and moves away from the rack. "Maybe this time she'll give the farm a chance."

Cherry gets our attention. "I'm ready to check out. You find anything?"

"I'm going to get these scarfs. Annie's done too." As we walk to the counter I speak over my shoulder. "So, your only other grandkids are Adam's kids, right?"

Annie ambles behind me. "Yes, he and Leesa have three. They're ten, seven, and four. Leesa works from home, so I only fill in when she needs a hand. She's a bookkeeper, and she's knee-deep in finalizing all the reports from Shrimp Fest."

Cherry takes her bag off the counter to make room for my scarves. She laughs. "I feel like I'm just now recovering from Shrimp Fest. The heat wave that weekend had us jumping at the hospital. People were dropping like flies!"

"So, it's not usually this hot in May?" I pull out three dollars and pay the young man behind the counter.

"No," Cherry says. "Not like this. And for it to start Shrimp Fest weekend was just bad timing. Folks walking in the sun, not drinking water, and the large crowds…"

"Wonder if the heat had anything to do with that lady Amanda dying," I say.

"Possibly," Cherry says.

Annie shrugs as she turns. "The heat and

then Shrimp Fest is a lot of work, and she was one of the top dogs. Lord knows if I was in charge of that thing I'd have a heart attack."

"I was worried about the heat in the house making someone sick this weekend," I admit as we walk toward the door. "Actually, as sad as it made me, I completely understood Jared wanting to take Sadie and Carver to a hotel. We have to bite the bullet and look into central air conditioning. But can you imagine what it will cost in that place?"

They nod sympathetically. Annie comes to a standstill and digs in her purse. "I'm putting my sunglasses on before I go out there and blind myself again."

"Good idea," I say, and Cherry and I sift through our bags to find our sunglasses. "Might make it not feel so hot."

Cherry smirks. "Doubt that. So, come on, you and Craig didn't talk at all this weekend? Nothing?"

Maybe it's being well-fed and relaxed, maybe it's being able to hide behind my sunglasses, maybe it's just that I'm putting off going out in the heat, but whatever it is, I spill. "He wants us to"—I pause, then shrug and finish—"work it out."

Annie stops with her hand on the door and exclaims, "Work it out? How is that going to happen with him practically living in South Florida? Long-distance counseling over Skype?"

"Oh no," I say. Sudden tears cause me to blink rapidly behind my glasses. "Work out a divorce."

Annie's mouth drops open, then closes. Then it opens again. When a lady pushes on the door from the outside, Annie yelps and jumps back. The lady comes in as we move out of the way. I push forward and lead the three of us outside, where we move about a yard down the sidewalk and gather again.

Cherry side-hugs me, and still holding me in her one arm, she groans. "Divorce, ugh."

Annie nods, her mouth still deciding on opening or closing. She's rarely at a loss for words, and it makes me laugh in spite of everything. "Poor Annie. I'm sorry. It just popped out." A ragged sigh comes from deep inside. "But that's how it happened to me too."

"Oh honey," she moans as she pulls me into a full-on hug, the only kind she gives. "I'm so sorry." She looks at her watch. "I have to go. Leesa's expecting me." But then she jumps back and grabs onto us. "I know! The kids will just be playing in the pool. Come with me. You can follow me there." She steps off the curb at the same time that she presses her car fob.

Cherry and I look at each other, then at our friend hustling across the hot pavement. Cherry yells, "Can we swim?"

"Sure, of course." Her silver curls shining in the sun, Annie turns. "Do you have your suits? I'll send you the address if you just want to meet there."

"My suit's in the car from the Y earlier," Cherry says, then turns to me. "You are coming, right?"

"I don't want to swim, but, um, okay."

Cherry pulls me off the curb with her. "Hurry and we can just follow Annie."

My car is sweltering, but I realize I'm shivering as I turn the ignition. That's the first time I've said the "D" word out loud. Now they want to talk about it.

It's all about to become real.

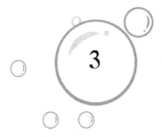

3

"I don't think your daughter-in-law was thrilled we showed up with you," Cherry says as she sits at the foot of a lounge chair.

Annie turns from where she's standing at the edge of the pool to face us. "I got used to Leesa not being thrilled with anything I do years ago. She disapproves, and I act like I'm too stupid to realize it. It's our thing." She grins, waggles her eyebrows, and turns back to check on her granddaughters racing across the pool. "Good job, Meghan. Way to go, Katie." The girls come up across from us, sputtering and jerking up their goggles, asking who won.

I move to sit down on the lounge next to Cherry's. She's scooted back to sit, and her legs are out in front of her. She has on those

23

cute tennis shoes with the crisscross straps and long, khaki shorts. Her hair is dark and short, her jewelry minimal, and she just looks like a nurse you can trust.

As I scoot back, I also put my legs up. My poor Midwestern legs with their first sunburn of the season. We got to spend time at the beach over the weekend, and I guess I forgot how hot the sun gets here. We kept Carver slathered in sunscreen, but me? Not so much, apparently. Annie chooses a chair and drags it from the table to sit near us.

"Thank goodness A.J. is taking a nap. Gives us a chance to just chill watching the girls." With a look at me she adds, "And talk." She settles in the chair. "So, he actually said 'divorce'?"

"Yes. And even worse, I think he said something about it to the boys. They went on a fishing trip one morning. All the boys, not just Craig and our two, but the sons-in-law as well. So you know that means my daughters must've heard *something.*"

Cherry shakes her head. "Did they say anything?"

"Not really. It was just the way they acted. And Craig went on and on about how wonderful it is in South Florida. How this place isn't really Florida and how they'll love it when they visit him there."

"But would your daughter that you talk to so much—Erin, isn't it? Wouldn't she have mentioned it to you?" Annie asks.

"Her husband might not have told her yet. She seemed sad, but that could've been about getting in their car for the drive back to St. Louis. It was a chaotic weekend." I sigh and watch the girls diving to the bottom of the pool to pick up brightly colored rings.

"But what did he say to *you?*" Cherry asks.

With a deep pull of air, my chest swells, and I push out the words. "Nothing really new. Well, except for the actual word. But I haven't been exactly honest." I pause and close my eyes to get through what I need to say. "I haven't told you that we, Craig and I, have been in this space for quite a while. Even before we got here. He wanted to turn down the inheritance. Not take the house, not move. We had been in counseling for a while, and from the beginning he said he thought we should separate. That there really wasn't any need for us to keep playing house together once all the kids were gone."

With that deluge I'm empty. There's silence, and when I open my eyes they are both staring at me.

Annie shakes her head. "Oh my! No, you did not tell us all that." She looks at the pool and shouts, "Girls, one at a time! Don't jump in on top of each other."

"Seriously? He didn't want to move here? Didn't want the house at all?" Cherry asks, her face scrunched up and her voice low. "Do you mean this whole thing was more, uh, *your* idea?"

"No. I mean it was completely my idea." Staring down at the arm of the chair, which I'm grasping to keep me sitting here talking, I admit it all. "I forced it. Forced the whole thing. I honestly thought if we got down here I'd have him to myself. No job, no kids, nothing but us and the beach. A second honeymoon. A new start. That's why I didn't ask any questions about the inheritance, didn't even want to read the papers. How I missed the whole having to stay in the house for five years. I just wanted to get down here and get started on our new beginning."

Now we're all silently staring at the girls swimming. Honestly, what can my friends say to that?

Cherry reaches over and pats my arm eventually. "That actually clears things up. The whole thing makes more sense."

"I know. Sorry."

"Grandma?" says a sweet voice behind us. Carrying a white blanket and a Lion King stuffed animal, a little boy squeezes through the cracked-open sliding door.

"Hey, honey. Come here and sit on Grandma's lap." He doesn't even give me and Cherry a look, but heads right to Annie's open arms. She gathers him up, whispering into his blond hair. He snuggles into her, and she looks up at us with a grin. "Sweetest thing God ever made."

The girls come dripping from the pool. "Grandma, A.J.'s up, so can we have a snack now?"

"In a minute. Y'all remember my friends, Miss Jewel and Miss Cherry? I'm sure you've met them before."

"Yeah. Hi," the younger sister says with a quick wave in our direction. "Momma said we could have ice cream sandwiches since you're here and you'd probably give them to us anyway." Her eyes twinkle, and her smile says she knows she wasn't supposed to say that.

"Katie Ann, you little rat," her grandmother says, and we can see where Katie gets her twinkle and her smile. "Meghan, dry off and go get one for each of you. Katie, you stay out here."

A.J. plows off her lap. "No sammich, I want a popsicle!" Then he screams, "Meghan! Red popsicle!"

"Mercy!" Annie says. "Y'all are acting like heathens in front of my friends. Let me up," she says as she pushes him away from her knees. Directing the girls she adds, "You two sit at the table over there. I'll go inside." Looking at us as she walks, she asks, "Y'all want an ice cream sandwich or a popsicle? I'm having one."

Cherry shrugs and with a laugh says, "Sure. An ice cream sandwich sounds great."

I say, "No, thanks," then laugh with her as Annie takes the kids to the table outside the kitchen door. With the circus relocated, I ask Cherry, "So, what do you think? Am I just an idiot for holding out and forcing this whole move?"

"Do you feel like an idiot?"

Annie sticks her head out the kitchen door and yells, "Don't say anything important until I get back out there!"

"Well then." Cherry jumps up from her lounge. "I'm putting on my suit so I can swim some laps after I eat my ice cream." She grabs her bag and jogs into the kitchen.

Alone, I look around. The house isn't very big and is in a neighborhood of similar one-story homes. The backyard is mostly the pool with an apron of grass around it, then a tall privacy fence. Mature trees hang over the fence, and the age of the houses says the neighborhood has been here a few decades at least. It feels very eighties and perfect for raising a family. Adam, Annie's son, is a manager down at the marina and has always lived on Sophia Island. I wonder if his wife is also a local.

Annie and Cherry have just come back outside along with all three kids, who of course had to pick out their own treat, when they suddenly turn to look inside the house. Annie slides the door back open. "You're home early."

Her daughter-in-law comes outside, and if she didn't look happy when she left, she looks even more unhappy now. She has on a gray, stretch knit dress with low-heeled, black, slip-on shoes. She kicks off the shoes and puts on a smile to say hi to the kids. They give her little attention as they are focused on their melting snacks. She turns around and marches over to sit in the chair Annie had been in earlier. "Wait until you hear what's happened," she says to her mother-in-law, who sits on the bottom of Cherry's lounge while Cherry sits on the top of it.

"Should we leave?" I ask, but Leesa runs her hands through her thick, light-brown, shoulder-length hair.

"No, not at all. I'm so mad I don't care if people aren't supposed to know."

"Know what?" Annie asks. "Did you finish your work?"

"No, I didn't finish, and who knows when I will. They've shut it all down. All of it. And of course I don't get paid until I turn in the final report. Lord knows when that'll be now. I didn't even know Amanda Raines had a son."

"Wait, Amanda Raines. The woman who died?" Cherry asks through a mouthful of ice cream sandwich.

Annie and Leesa nod. Annie says, "Amanda wasn't from here. She moved here, oh, a while back, but she didn't raise her kids here. What's her son got to do with anything?"

"He's got an investigation started. He says there was funny business going on with the books from the Shrimp Festival."

"Well, that's not good. Why does he think that?" Annie says.

"He says his mother told him about it. Told him toward the end of the festival that she couldn't hide it anymore and was going to take everything to the police station as soon as the festival was over."

Annie's eyebrows dip, and she screws up her face. "But, but you have the books. So she didn't do that, right?"

Cherry pauses, holding the last piece of her ice cream sandwich in front of her mouth between two sticky fingers. "Because she died, right?"

Leesa shrugs and deepens her frown. "Who knows? I got them the week after the festival, and I haven't seen anything suspicious." She bristles. "All I do know is that no one better try and hang anything on me."

Cherry pops the last bite into her mouth, then stands up and walks to the pool's edge. Bending for her dive, she looks back at us. "All *I* know is it sounds mighty convenient, her dying like that."

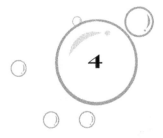

4

"You're back!" I greet Eden when I walk in my front door to find her in the kitchen.

"Yes, ma'am. Just stocking the fridge." Eden—Annie's son's girlfriend, barista at the local coffee shop, and my roommate—has dark red hair. She's been living at my house since the end of April, but she moved to her folks' this weekend while my family was visiting.

"You know how I feel about being called ma'am." I sit at the kitchen table in front of the tiny window air conditioner.

Eden turns around, a tub of yogurt in her hand, and leans against the counter. "How come it's only folks not from the South that it bothers? First you, and then I noticed it this weekend with some of the tourists at work."

"'Cause you guys grow up with it being a sign of respect, so you don't associate it with age. The rest of the world thinks it's just for old people. Might want to remember that. Could impact your tips. Goodness, the air conditioning feels good."

"It's still so hot out there. Wish we'd get some rain." She comes to sit at the table with her opened yogurt. "So glad to have a day off and so glad to get moved back in. Aiden was supposed to have the day off, too, but just as we were headed out to lunch, he got called over to the station."

"What's going on?"

"Something with the Shrimp Festival. His sister-in-law was involved, so they thought it'd be best if he came in for a minute." She sits up to look out the side window. "Speak of the devil, there he is now."

Yes, we can actually see out the windows now. The Mantelle Mansion was built in 1888 and has been in the family ever since. However, until Craig inherited it last year, it sat empty for ten years after the owner, Cora-belle Mantelle Hocking, gave up her recluse status and moved into a senior citizen home, though some say it was a mental institution.

Craig had completely forgotten about his great-aunt and was surprised, and not very happy, to learn about his inheritance. He didn't get any happier when we got here in January and found it dark, dirty, and encased in wild, junglelike bushes. Eden's father arranged to have the bushes trimmed back in April, and the cut branches were finally removed a couple of weeks ago. Then I paid a young man who also works with Eden at Sophia Coffee to pressure-wash the windows. He couldn't do a very thorough job, as we realized the caulking was being blasted out, but he managed to clean off the top layer of grime. (Missing window caulk is another reason I haven't looked into real air conditioning.)

"Hey, I'm back!" Aiden, Annie's youngest son, calls as he comes in the back door and down the hallway to the kitchen. "Oh, hey, Miss Jewel."

"Hi, Aiden. You can have my seat in front of the air conditioner. I'm heading upstairs to get changed."

"Oh, no, ma'am. I can't sit. Just came by to tell Eden that I have to work." With his hands on the back of her chair, he smiles at me, but I can see he has more to say. Not to me.

I jump up. "I need to get changed anyway. Surely you can visit with Eden for a minute." Climbing the stairs I hear him pulling out the chair I'd been sitting in. He'll fill Eden in on what's going on, and then she'll fill me in.

We have a system.

In my bedroom, I close the door behind me. It's stiflingly hot up here by this time in the afternoon. Clicking on the standing fan in the corner, I stand in front of it to undress. Even though my bedroom faces the street, its windows are buried in the tree limbs, and I don't have to worry about closing the curtains to keep out prying eyes. One of the side windows has a palm tree right outside it, and this spring the wind clapping the big palm fronds became one of my all-time favorite sounds. Now, though, I can't imagine opening the windows because at night it's hotter out there than in here, even without air conditioning. I had Aiden move the window air conditioner from this room into the room Carver and his parents were going to be in for the long weekend. Since Aiden is working today, I have another night with just the fan before he can move the window unit back. There are four rooms on this floor, so I guess I could sleep in the room with the air conditioner down the hall, but moving is such a hassle. Besides, I really like this room.

My room is the only bedroom without dark, falling-down, floral wallpaper. The walls here are white plaster, and while it's cracked and there are even a few places where chunks have fallen out, the room is so bright and open. Without the thick branches outside, it would probably be too bright with all the sunshine, but it feels like a tree house. Craig wants total darkness for sleeping, so he demanded thick curtains, but I dragged my feet. As a matter of fact he used that as an excuse when he finally moved all of his things down the hall.

My floors are an aged, darkened wood, and while I'd originally planned to find a big rug to cover them, I've come to appreciate the coolness of the floors. The connected bathroom is small, with a tiny tub I have to step up into to use the attached shower nozzle. Of course that's only after I've pulled the curtains around the tub on both sides. So, that's not all that great, but I can manage. Taking a bath, however, I can't really manage as the tub is barely long enough for me to sit in, much less stretch out my legs. Luckily I've never been a bath person. Besides, there is a larger, old-fashioned tub in the hall bathroom if I really want a soak.

In the hall, I step around a laundry basket outside the next bedroom, the one where my boys slept over the weekend. Sticking my head in the door, I see Eden taking sheets off the twin beds. "It's too hot to do laundry in the afternoon," I say. "Leave that until later."

She shakes her head. "Figured I'd strip the beds and at least get everything downstairs. Between the towels and all the sheets, it's going to take several loads."

"So, what's up with Aiden?" I go into the room to take pillowcases off the pillows she's stacked in a chair.

"Something about the Shrimp Fest money and Miss Raines. But he doesn't think it's anything. Her son is just making a fuss." She picks up a load and carries it to the hall.

I follow her and toss the pillowcases into the basket. Eden says, "I hear he's a writer. Think his imagination has gotten away with him?"

"Probably. And he's grieving. I mean, Miss Raines wasn't that old, was she?"

"No. I don't think so." She picks up the basket, and I move out of her way.

But then she stops in front of me. "Um, I'm borrowing an air conditioner from my folks. It was in a rental house they used to own, and it's just sitting in their storage unit. Dad is bringing it out tonight to put in my room, and then we'll move the one in that corner room back to your room, okay?" Without waiting for an answer she walks past me and starts down the long staircase.

I cringe and follow. "Okay. I'm sorry you're having to do all that. I've got to find out about putting in air. Do your folks know someone?"

She stops halfway down the stairs and looks back at me. "Of course they do. But do not ask my dad. You remember how it was with the branches laying in the yard for weeks? That's how all his friends work."

"Good point." We go straight to the laundry room, which is past the kitchen, down the hall toward the back door. It's a dark little space that looks like it originally was part of a room used for serving or storing food, but when indoor plumbing was added they used half this room for the bathroom and half for the laundry room. Craig's aunt didn't seem to worry about how the house was laid out or if things flowed naturally. It appears she stuck things wherever was easiest.

Just past the laundry is Craig's office, a large room with tall windows. I think it was supposed to be a dining room—or maybe a sitting room? I guess the air would flow well with the large windows. Across the hall from Craig's office is a room that up until a few weeks ago was packed with furniture, but now is the only bedroom downstairs. "Erin and Paul stayed down here," I say. "I'll get the sheets in there." Eden cleaned it out before Memorial Day, and it's a good-sized room with a bed and still more furniture than it needs. It served its purpose, though. Erin liked not having to climb the stairs, and since she's having trouble sleeping during her pregnancy, I thought she could wander the downstairs or watch TV at night.

"Come on," I say to Eden when I add those sheets to the pile in the laundry room. "Let's get a drink. You can tell me the rest of what Aiden had to say." I head into the kitchen and pour two glasses of water.

"Okay, but first tell me how the weekend went." She plops down beside me at the table with a bag of chilled grapes.

"We had fun. The kids loved the beach and the water sports. Paul golfed; Erin had morning, noon, and evening sickness, it seemed. Carver stayed with his folks out at the beach, so that was a disappointment, but they said the house was too hot." As if to testify to the truth of that, we turn our faces to the cold air blowing at us from the window unit.

Eden's parents own a tattoo shop, and she's their best advertisement for tattoos of the floral and leafy variety. As she cools down, the flower on her cheek fades to a softer pink.

"How was it staying at your parents' this weekend?" I ask.

She laughs, then rolls her eyes. "They are so happy in that little apartment above the shop, but it's tiny! They've always acted like kids, but now they are almost ridiculous."

When her parents moved their shop downtown, they also rented the apartment above the shop. They sold the house Eden was raised in, which was when she came to live with me and help me sort things out in this house. I had no idea how much I'd enjoy her company and how much help she'd truly be. I'm glad her parents' place is tiny. I guess I'm also glad they're happy. I try, but I can't hold back my sigh as I lament, "Must be nice."

She squints at me and then reaches out to pat my arm. "Things weren't better with you and your husband?"

"Nope. I guess we're just going to let things go on like this for now, him living down there where his project is and me living up here in his family home, but I'm bored talking about all that. So, the son of this woman that died, is he an author I've heard of?"

She pulls off some more grapes. "He has books in the bookstore downtown, and I guess he's done some signings here. Aiden said folks at the police station read his books. Guess that's some of why they're taking him seriously."

"What's his name? Let's google him."

She picks up her phone. "Let me text Aiden and ask."

While we're waiting my phone rings, and I get it off the counter where I'd plugged it in. "It's Tamela," I tell Eden, then turn back to the phone. "Hi there."

"Hi. Are you home? Can Hert and I stop in? We're just around the corner."

"Sure. What's up?"

"We'll be right there. Bye."

She hangs up before I can say goodbye. "Tamela and her husband are headed over here. I don't know him. Do you?"

Eden wrinkles her nose. "I don't think so. What do they want? Oh, and the writer guy's name is Timothy Raines."

"That doesn't sound familiar," I say as I

walk toward the front door. "Tamela's here already." By the time I get to the front door, they are walking up the front steps, so I meet them on the porch. There is another man with them. "Hi."

"Hey, Jewel. Sorry to just drop in like this. Have you ever met Hert?" A man just a little bit taller than Tamela steps forward with his hand out. Tamela is petite, and her husband is too. "No, I don't think we have met."

He has a big smile and no hair. "Nice to meet you, Jewel." We shake, and then he steps to the side. "This is my friend Tim."

"Oh! Hello." I reach out to shake Tim's hand. An attractive man in dress pants and a button-down shirt with rolled-up sleeves bounds up the final steps, shakes my hand, and then strides past all of us to the open door.

"So this is the Mantelle Mansion," he says as he steps across the threshold with the three of us following. "Oh, hello," he greets Eden when she walks out of the kitchen. He strides across the room toward her, hand out to shake as Hert apologizes.

"Sorry about that. It's just Tim's always talked about this house. I guess you could say you're kind of on his bucket list." Hert laughs as he follows his friend, then also reaches out his hand to Eden.

Tamela exclaims. "You two! Calm down." She catches up to her husband and grabs his arm. "Eden, this is my husband, Hert, and his friend Timothy Raines."

Eden and I both say, "Oh!" then she tucks her hand so that she's holding her phone behind her. I bet she'd just googled him on it.

"You're the author?" I ask.

"Yes," he says as he looks around the room. "And this... this house is the setting of my new book."

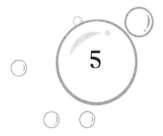

5

"This house? My house?"

He cocks his head at me. "Your husband is the one who inherited it, correct?"

"Yes, but…"

"He works down south," Tamela answers for me, then prods her husband forward. "Hert, explain to Jewel. Please."

"Of course. Jewel, is it okay if I call you that? I mean, I feel like I know you from Tamela talking about all of y'all." He's bouncing on the balls of his feet and grins at me when I nod. "Timothy is, as you know, an author, and we met several months ago when he did a signing here. I'm interested in writing a book, so we've kept in touch."

Turning to keep an eye on Mr. Raines as he wanders around the big, open living space,

I say in his direction, "I'm sorry to hear about your mother."

His shoulders slump, then bound back into place as he stops to stretch and look up the staircase. Slowly he turns to us. "Yes. Thank you." He shakes his head and runs a hand through his sandy brown hair. He looks to be in his forties, and as he rubs his chin I can see gray mixed in his day's growth of beard. "Seeing this place has taken my mind off Mom for a moment. Plus, I'd like to forget that debacle at the police station. Such idiots!"

I see, and feel, Eden bristle, so I move forward. "I'm sure they're trying to help. I mean, I know for a fact they called in some officers for extra duty to figure things out."

He's perceptive, and his eyes shift from me to Eden. "They did? Who? Why?"

Eden's eyes pop open, and she takes a step back. "I don't know. I have to go," she blurts, and she turns back to the kitchen.

Tamela, in her schoolteacher's voice, interrupts. "Mr. Raines—Timothy. Let's sit down." Our guest claims my leather lounge chair, so I take a straight-backed chair while Tamela and Hert find other seats.

Mr. Raines sits on the end of the lounge and leans forward, elbows on his knees. His focus is on me. "So you believe the police are taking me seriously? Can I ask why you would think that?"

"Well, uh, I know a police officer who was supposed to have the day off but has been called in because of your concerns."

"Good. Good to know. Did you know my mother?"

"No. I haven't lived here long."

"Yes." He nods. "I know. I've tried to get into this place for at least the past year. When it was handed over and the papers were finally registered, I tried contacting your husband. He's not very good at communication is my unvarnished opinion."

"Mine too," Tamela murmurs.

I smirk at her, but then shrug at Mr. Raines. "You're probably right."

"I'd even asked my mother to simply show up, knock on your door, but she said that's not how things are done down here. You're not from here, though, are you?"

"No. The Midwest. I wish I'd had the chance to meet your mother."

Hert speaks up. "If Tamela actually listened to me she might've made the connection earlier."

My friend rolls her eyes, and I can't help but smile. I do seem to remember Tamela mentioning how much Hert talks. She says to him, "I had no idea your famous author friend was Amanda's son. I just didn't know. But we're here now."

The famous author has dropped his head, and he's staring at the floor. "Yes. Here we are now. My mother should not be dead. She was fanatical about her health. It's all about that damned festival." He suddenly stands. "I should know. I write books about this very thing! Sex and money. It's always about sex and money!" he says as he strides through us toward the front door.

Tamela, Hert, and I meet eyes. We stand and then follow Mr. Raines into the entry-way. "Sex and money?" I ask loudly.

He whips around. "You don't think she was taking the money for herself, do you? No. It had to be for a man."

Tamela tries to laugh. "Amanda? Why, I don't think so. I mean, it's an awfully small island, and I've never heard anything like that."

Hert eases toward his friend. "Aww, Tim. You don't want to start rumors about some-thing like that. This place is crazy for rumors. Your mother was a good woman. Lots of people loved her."

Taking a deep breath, Mr. Raines squints

as he looks at Hert, then Tamela. "I agree with what you are both saying, but I also know what my mother told me." He turns toward the door again, and I step forward to open it. It felt hot in the house before, but now the boiling afternoon air comes flowing in. They walk into the heat, and I come up behind them as they descend the wooden steps, Hert and Tamela thanking me as they move along.

At the bottom of the stairs, Mr. Raines looks along the row of palm trees that leads to the street, then turns back to look up at me. "I hope you will allow me to visit again when I'm not so preoccupied. I'll get your number from Mrs. Stout. Just getting to be inside for a few moments has helped clear my mind. Thank you very much, Mrs. Mantelle." He ends with a flourish of his arm and hand.

"Oh, Mr. Raines," I say, which makes him turn back toward me. "Can I ask what it is that your mother told you? About the money and the, uh, sex?"

He looks at the palm trees again, but this time he leans his head back to look up where their massive heads punctuate the blue sky. There's no wind to make them sway or whip, but he stares at them anyway for a bit longer. I'm embarrassed.

"I'm sorry. I shouldn't have asked. Never mind. It was nice to meet—"

"No, it's not that. I'm just deciding how this should all be laid out. How it should unroll." He slowly, intentionally steps to the bottom stair, near where Hert and Tamela still stand. "Yes, you may ask. My mother told me she stole a little over a hundred thousand dollars from the Shrimp Festival in the past few years."

Three sets of blinking eyes stare back at him. As I look to see what Tamela and Hert think, I see their mouths are slack like mine. Then Hert shakes his head and mumbles, "Impossible."

Mr. Raines smirks, then swings back around and begins walking along the palm trees toward the street. Tamela shoves her husband. "Where is he going? Go talk to him!"

Hert jumps and then runs after the man. She and I stare after them. Hert yells, "Tamela! You bring the car!"

She frowns, shakes her head, and then walks to their car.

"So that's the famous author," I hear someone say behind me. Eden waits just inside the open front door. She clicks her tongue and crosses her arms. "I think he's crazy, and believe me, I know crazy."

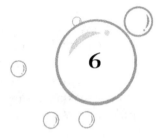

6

"He's crazy. There is no way a hundred thousand dollars were taken from the festival," Lucy states as she shuffles papers at her desk.

I'm sitting across from her, having just told her about my recent visitor. At lunch earlier she told me to stop by her office for a copy of Sophia Beach's Downtown Historic District guidelines for house renovations. She doesn't work specifically with the planning or zoning commissions but said she has anything I might need to learn about renovating in her files. Which I believe after seeing this place.

We're on the second floor of a building a block off Centre Street. The receptionist is actually tucked into an alcove at the top of the steps. She pointed me down the old,

narrow, brick hallway to the office at the
end, and there I found Lucy behind a large,
old-fashioned desk. The wall behind her is
also exposed brick, but the brick can only be
seen above the impressive line of white filing
cabinets. Two small but comfortable chairs
covered in jade-green fabric face her desk.
I'm seated in the one farthest from the door,
next to a tall window looking out over the
library and its parking lot. Another window
is across the room at the end of the row of
filing cabinets. The non-brick walls are a soft,
peachy pink and covered with framed post-
ers of Sophia Beach activities like the Shrimp
Festival. As a matter of fact, the walls are the
color of cooked shrimp.

"Here's everything you need," she says,
holding up a handful of brochures, leaflets,
and sheets of paper. "I'll get you a folder to
put it all in."

"All that's for me? I just want to find out
about putting in some air conditioning."

She closes the folder and looks up at me
over the top of her reading glasses. "Own-
ing a home in a historic district is not for
the faint of heart. You really need to decide
what you're going to do with it before you
get too deep into renovations. *Expensive* renovations."

I take the folder and stand with a shiver.

She softens her stern look with a bit of a smile. "Sorry about how cold it is in here. We had a meeting earlier in the conference room, and they turned the thermostat down to the artic setting."

"No problem. I think I'm getting used to my house being so hot that I freeze whenever I'm in air conditioning. Thanks for putting all this together."

She stands up too. "Give me a minute and I'll walk down with you. I have a meeting tonight, so I'm going home to have dinner with Birdie." Birdie is Lucy's mother. They live together in their family home on the beach.

Lucy steps into her slip-on heels and picks up her purse and satchel. She's always so well put together. Her off-white jacket and skirt show off her tan, and I only know her brown turtleneck is sleeveless because she had her jacket off at lunch. Her streaked blonde hair is styled to look effortless. With a toss of her head like she's leaving her office problems behind, she points me toward the hall. "So, tell me more about Amanda's son. I knew he was an author, but I don't believe I ever met him." She turns off the light and closes her door behind us. "Amanda, sorry to say, tended to drone on and on about things, so I'm assuming she talked about him, but who knows. I could've missed it in all that droning. I'm going to download one of his books tonight."

"But you don't think what he said about her taking that money is right?"

"Absolutely not." We wave to the receptionist, who is talking on the phone about the tide times, and we turn to walk downstairs. "Maybe he's just drumming up stuff for this next book of his. You said it's set in your house?" She stops at the bottom and looks at me. "Do you think he means to set it here on Sophia Island?"

"I don't know. Maybe?" On the sidewalk I turn toward Centre since I'd walked from the house.

"You want a ride?" Lucy asks. "Actually, I'm a couple of blocks down this way. By the time you walk there, you'd be practically home."

"Thanks, but no. I think I might stop into the bookstore and look up our author friend. I've never actually met an author before!" We laugh and wave to each other as we part.

The sun is still high but on its way down to another summer sunset over the river. The sidewalks are getting busier as folks have come off the beaches, taken showers, and

gotten dressed. Now the hunt for dinner begins. The restaurants are still empty, but it
won't be long before there are lines outside
the popular ones. The ice cream and fudge
shop doesn't have a line yet, and as I walk
past it I take a deep breath. It always smells so
delicious, whether they are spreading a vat of
fudge out on the marble table in the window
or ladling out my new favorite, pralines. The
sugary candies are full of meaty pecans. The
sweet candy slowly dissolves while you chew
on the pecans. If there's no line when I finish
in the bookstore, I'll come get a couple.

Eden deserves a treat.

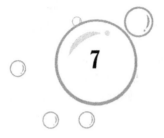

7

Red and white checks greet me from behind the words "The Book Store," which are painted in gold, scripted lettering on the front window of the downtown bookshop. The red and white checks are old-fashioned picnic blankets on which beautiful cookbooks are displayed. Large pictures of colorful food, mostly in outdoor settings, follow through on the picnic theme. Escaping a wicker hamper is a loaf of bread, the neck of a wine bottle, and linen napkins printed with sailboats. When I look beyond the appealing display, I see a number of people shopping inside, so I move to the door and join them.

There are books everywhere, which is to be expected on the shelves covering the brick walls, but they are also displayed much as the cookbooks in the front window are: on every surface and at every level. The result is very accessible and very appealing.

"Welcome to The Book Store," the man behind the counter says in my direction as he rings up the purchases of the family in front of him. He only gives me a quick smile before going back to his work, so I move past the counter toward the shelves. We'd brought Carver in here, as the children's area is as appealing as the rest of the store. Even though he was quickly ready to move on to the ice cream we'd promised him, we ended up with a bag of books for him, several of which I kept to begin my grandma library.

A woman comes out of the office door as I pass, so I ask her about Timothy Raines's books. "Oh, let me see," she says as she leads me back to the front, then up a couple of steps to a small raised area. "Here you go. Are you looking for one in particular?"

"No, I just heard about him and wanted to check out his books."

She smiles. "I'd get the first one, *Dual Threat*. It did quite well." She adds a wrinkle of her nose. "The others? Not so much." When someone calls out to her from the counter area, she lifts her head and answers, "Coming." Pulling out the book she'd mentioned and handing it to me, she says, "Just let me know if you need anything else," as she moves toward the steps.

It's a big hardback book. I open the front cover to read the summary, and it doesn't sound like anything I'd like. There's a bomb somewhere on the East Coast, and the hero, a recently fired cop, has to find it before it goes off. There's a ransom involved and a kidnapped daughter of a scientist. I'm guessing the woman in the red dress showing a lot of leg on the cover is the damsel in distress. Why do women always get kidnapped in revealing dresses or lingerie?

There's a chair near the front window that a young woman leaves, so I hurry to claim it and settle in. I'm not paying for a hardback book I won't like. It shouldn't take more than a few minutes to thumb through it and read the author's biography.

However, the next time I look up, it's almost dark outside and the store is much quieter. I'm also a good ways into the book. Blinking, I can't believe how this book sucked me in. I'm also finding it hard to believe I'm in a bookstore on Sophia Island when just a moment ago I was in a warehouse in Savannah, Georgia, hiding from a man with a gun.

Guess I'll buy the book.

My stomach rumbles, and I realize that's what interrupted my reading. At the front counter it rumbles again, and the woman who'd helped me earlier laughs. "You sure were engrossed in your reading. It's good, isn't it?"

"I didn't think I'd like it at all, but it just grabbed me."

"He does signings here occasionally."

"Yes, I know. I actually met him earlier today."

"Tim is in town?" The man who'd been behind the counter earlier steps up behind me.

"Yes. His mother, well, his mother lived here. She died last week."

"That's right," the man says, shaking his head. "I haven't seen anything about her funeral in the paper yet, but maybe she's not being buried here." He looks to the woman putting my book in a bag and explains. "He's not from Sophia Island, but his mother moved here several years ago. What a shame he had to come back so soon, unless he didn't leave. Maybe he stayed to take care of his mother if she was sick?"

I take my bag and hold it against my stomach, which is threatening another loud rumble. "He's been here recently?"

"Not here in the store, but I ran into him just two weeks ago out on the beach. I'd've missed that it was him, but his hat blew off and I chased it down for him. I tried to ask him why he wasn't doing a book signing, but he didn't want to talk." He rocks on his heels and preens a bit. "Being the one who lines up the book signings, I know how to talk to authors, but sometimes they just don't want to be bothered. Hopefully he'll stop in while he's in town."

I nod and step around him to get to the front door. He's obviously a talker, and I'm obviously starving to death. "Nice to meet you, but I need to go," I say as I turn.

"Hey! If you talk to him again can you tell him we'd love to have him stop in? At least to sign the copies on the shelf."

"Sure. Thanks again." Then, pushing out through the heavy wood-and-glass door, I'm on the sidewalk, where the smell of food reinforces my hunger. White lights in the trees twinkle over the sidewalks full of people, and I cross to an area underneath a big tree along Centre Street to decide which direction would be best for walking home. Then I spot the candy and ice cream store and remember the pralines. There's a line, but it's not too long. I hurry in that direction.

Besides, pralines for dinner means I can keep reading.

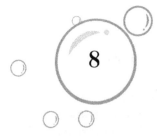

8

The phone wakes me, but the pounding on the door downstairs gets me out of bed. I see it's Craig on the phone, but it stops ringing while I'm pulling on shorts and a T-shirt in the bright morning sunshine. I can call him back, but the pounding on the door sounds like the house might be on fire. I grab my phone and head out of my room and down the hall.

Eden's door is open, and seeing as it's nine thirty, she's already up and at work. I stayed up late last night reading. Too late apparently.

I pull open the front door to see a man heading away from me, down the front steps. "Can I help you?" I ask.

He turns around. "Mrs. Mantelle? Your

husband said you were home, but I'd about given up." Bounding up the stairs, he smiles and then holds his hand out to me. "Victor Morrison." In his other hand he holds a clipboard, and as we shake he waves it toward the shiny, red truck in my front yard. Two men take that as a signal to leave the back seat and join us.

We release hands. "My husband?" As if on cue my phone rings again. Without even looking at it, I stop the ringing. "What's going on?"

Mr. Morrison is older than me, but one of those polished men who exudes success. He's broad-shouldered, has a full head of dark hair streaked with gray only at the temples, and his navy dress pants and light blue golf shirt look starched. He also has a gold chain showing in the open neck of his shirt that matches an impressive watch on his wrist. He grimaces, then looks down at his clipboard. Still squinting, he looks back at me. "Let me guess. Your husband didn't tell you he called me?"

"No," I say as I fold my arms. "I assume he's calling to tell me about you now, but since you're already here, why don't you tell me?"

"Of course. Island Heat and Air is my

company. We're thirty-two years old, even though we've only been here on this island for ten years. Here's our brochure."

As I reach for the brochure, there's hope in my question. "Air? As in air conditioning?"

Mr. Morrison smiles and even laughs a bit at that. He's a man who's comfortable in his own skin and skilled at making everyone around him comfortable. "Yes, ma'am. I understand from Mr. Mantelle that is something you might be interested in?"

"Very! But I didn't realize my husband even—" I choke on the word "cared" and stumble a bit, substituting, "That he even knew it was hot." I cringe because that was stupid, but Mr. Morrison ignores it.

The men from the truck wait at the bottom of the stairs. "This is Hector and Pete," their boss says by way of introduction. "They'll be doing the survey for the estimate. I'm too old to do that these days." The men wave, nod, and smile, and then, at a nod from Mr. Morrison, they go back to the truck and begin gathering equipment.

"You mean you're actually going to start today? But aren't there things to deal with since we're in the historic district?"

"Why don't we go inside and talk?" He

moves toward the door, and I back up, then turn to lead him inside.

"Sure. That's a good idea. I haven't even had any coffee this morning. Come in." I hurry to the kitchen while he wanders around the living room. I ask loudly, "Can I make you some coffee?"

"Thank you, but no. What a magnificent home. I'm not from Sophia, but I've heard this house was basically abandoned before you and your husband got here."

"Yes, and now we're not sure what to do first."

He enters the kitchen as my coffee finishes, and I motion for him to sit at the kitchen table.

"Well, that's why your husband called me. These older homes are my specialty, and I know all about dealing with the historical design board. We follow all the regulations and take care of all permitting."

My groan of relief brings another chuckle from him as he sits down.

"That's amazing," I say. I pick up the folder I'd gotten yesterday but hadn't opened because I'd been obsessed with a certain book. "I got all this from my friend Lucy yesterday, and I have to admit it's overwhelming."

"Lucy Fellows?"

"Yes. Do you know... Never mind. Everyone knows Lucy."

"That's probably true. She is one busy lady," he says. "Lucy and I serve on the Shrimp Festival committee together."

"Oh really? I know you must be glad it's over and you can get back to some normalcy for a little while."

He leans back in his chair. "I don't really get much of a break since I'm the chairman."

"Of the whole thing?"

His laugh causes me to shut my mouth, which had dropped open in astonishment—or horror. "Yes, the whole thing!"

His men walking below us outside the window catch my eye, and I let out a big sigh of relief and toss the folder down on the table. "You've made my day. I didn't even know where to start."

"That's what I'm here for. I sent your husband some numbers on other jobs we've done along with folks to call for referrals. Plus, you can ask Lucy for her opinion. I should have the estimate ready by the day after tomorrow. I'll bring a copy here and also email it to Mr. Mantelle. Be sure and get some other estimates, but I believe you'll find we have the best reputation and a very competitive price. As I said before, I know all about the historic

board and how to get the permits through
quickly."

"Oh, I'm sure you know what you're doing. My husband works with contractors every day. He would only call the best." Mr.
Morrison stands up, and I do, too, as I take
his offered hand to shake.

"Nice to meet you, Mrs. Mantelle."

"You, too, Mr. Morrison."

"Please, call me Victor. Even if you choose
to go with another company, I'm sure we'll
be running into each other in the future."

"It does seem to be a small island. And
I'm Jewel." I follow him to the front door.
"Thanks for coming by. I look forward to
hearing from you. I suppose your men need
to come inside to look around."

"Yes, ma'am. If that's okay?"

"Oh, of course. I'll just leave the door
ajar, and you guys can come and go. I'll be in
the kitchen if you need anything."

He heads down the stairs with a wave.

I push the door almost shut and chuckle
all the way back to the kitchen and my coffee.

We're getting air conditioning!

"You'll love working with Victor," Lucy

promises again. "He and his wife, Martha, are sweethearts. They've only been here a little while but are so involved in everything!"

"A little while? He said ten years." I have the phone on speaker while I cut up an apple, and so her sigh is nice and loud.

"That's a little while to me. Boy, you really got on the stick. You seemed pretty hesitant yesterday when I gave you all the information. You must've been busy reading it all last night." Lucy's in her car, so she's also on speakerphone. She's waiting in the Dunkin' Donuts drive-through, and occasionally she talks to the people in the car in front of her under her breath. They are apparently taking too long.

"Well, actually, I didn't call him. Craig did."

"Really? So, did you and Craig talk or something? You didn't mention him yesterday. I thought this was kind of all in your lap."

"I thought so too. But Craig's always been pretty good at making sure things like this get done. Guess I should've thought of that. Apparently he was hot here last weekend too." I laugh, but I'm laughing alone.

"Well. If that's how y'all handle things."

There's definitely a pause. I get the feeling

Lucy isn't saying what she wants to say, so I decide it's time to hang up. "Okay, so you recommend Mr. Morrison. Enjoy your coffee, and I'll let you go."

"Sure thing. Besides, I might have to get out and figure out this humongous order they're trying to deal with in that car ahead of me. They've returned it, like, four times." She punctuates with a short horn blast, so I say goodbye and leave her to deal with things there.

Should I be aggravated that Craig is handling the air conditioning? That hadn't dawned on me, but Lucy sounded like it wasn't right. And now that I'm thinking about it, he did just spring this on me. Sure, he tried to call this morning, but he hasn't answered my calls since. And what if I don't want... Wait. Never mind. I desperately want air conditioning. But how are we paying for it? Shouldn't we be talking about the future of the house? Are we going to fix it up or just live in it "as is" until we can sell it?

Carrying my bowl of apple slices into the living room, I sit down and take a bite of one. Just thinking about all that makes me tired. Can you imagine how exhausting talking to Craig about it would be?

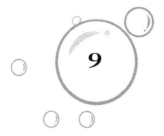

9

I've just put clean sheets on all the beds, sat down on my chaise, and put my feet up when Eden barrels in the front door. "We're getting air conditioning? Woohoo! The truck was just pulling out."

"They've been here for over two hours," I say. "You here for lunch?"

"Yep. I slept late this morning and had to hurry out without fixing anything to take with me. Have you eaten?" she yells from the kitchen.

"No, but I'm not hungry right now. Just thirsty. I think it's hotter now that I know we're getting air."

"Do you need a drink?"

"Nope, I have a glass of water. You eating in there?" I ask, but she walks into the living

73

room with her hands full so she doesn't need to answer.

She's balancing an open pouch of tuna and a stack of crackers along with a bottled iced tea. "When will they put it in?"

"Maybe as early as next week. We'll get the estimate Saturday, so we'll see. Do you know the company or the owner, Victor Morrison?"

"Not really. I mean, he's chair of the Shrimp Festival, so he's in the paper a lot and he comes in Sophia Coffee, but I don't know him. Speaking of the festival, I'm glad you're here because I couldn't wait to tell you. Looks like that crazy author guy might be right about his mother. Apparently the medical examiner thought something was off from the beginning, and that's why they haven't had her funeral."

"Did you get that from Aiden?"

"Yep. He said they're all stunned at the police station. Mrs. Raines's doctor works with the medical examiner and thought there was something wrong. She, the lady that died, apparently was something of a hypochondriac and like her son said was very diligent about her health and medications. Her doctor had already asked for additional blood tests and was waiting to see what they said." Eden's shoveling in her food and talking at the same time.

I hold out my hand. "Slow down. There's no hurry. Chew your food."

She grins. "Thanks, Mom." Then she takes a breath. "I do tend to bolt down my food." She chews, takes a sip of her tea, and pauses before she speaks. "Okay. So anyway, Charlie and Aiden went to talk to her doctor when they found all this out. Her son really lit a fire under the higher-ups yesterday. The doctor said he was getting ready to call them as there were problems with what they found."

"Like what?"

She had just put another loaded cracker in her mouth, so she shrugs and talks anyway. "Aiden didn't say. We were texting and he had to go into a meeting." She squints and looks beside me, at my chair. "Is that that guy's book?"

I move a bit and pull it out. She was out last night when I got home. I left her a praline on the counter, took my goodies upstairs, and spent the night reading. "Yes. It's so good."

"I don't like reading. I don't think I've ever read a book that big."

"It is big, but it moves so fast. I had no

idea I'd like it. As a matter of fact, I'm sitting right here in front of this fan and reading for the rest of the afternoon."

She gathers her things and stands. "I've got to get back to work. Thanks for the praline last night. Aiden of course ate most of it, but I've never been a big fan. I like fudge better."

"I'll remember that for next time."

"Aiden and I are having dinner with my parents tonight. You want to come?"

"I don't want to barge in."

"Oh, you're not. Mom is making her huge paella, and she told me to invite you. She only does it a couple of times a year, and it's so good. All kinds of seafood and it takes her all day. Besides, you'd get to see their apartment."

For less than a minute I think of another hot evening here. "Sure then, count me in."

Eden fills me in on the details while she puts things away in the kitchen. She's heading back out the door in a matter of minutes. With the air conditioning guys finally gone and Eden's whirlwind lunch over, the house seems to settle into the heat of the afternoon with a sigh.

I open my book and find myself back in Savannah, in the midst of the St. Patrick's

Day crowds, which hide a killer and my new love interest. I can't help but picture him as Tim Raines, though that might make it awkward if we meet again. We are rather involved, you know…

"There's no way Amanda would take anything like that," Eden's mother, Kerry, says from her seat on a high stool at the corner of the dinner table. The rest of us are beginning to slow down from shoveling in her delicious seafood paella.

We're crowded around a table in the kitchen of Eden's parents' downtown Sophia Beach apartment. We entered up an interior staircase in their tattoo parlor, Signs, because I told Eden and Aiden I'd never been inside one. It reminded me of a nail salon, with more technical equipment and more interesting décor, considering all the sample art, but with the same layout of tables and lights and chairs. There's also an outside staircase out back that comes up onto a small porch, and a sliding door that is between our table and the large, updated kitchen in the other rear corner of the apartment. Also on that side are the large bedroom and beautiful bathroom. The living room makes up the rest of the apartment, and all in all, it's much bigger than I'd imagined.

The dinner table is small, usually meant for just Kerry and her husband, Ted. There are three chairs that fit around the tile-topped table, which is set against a wall on one side. Aiden, Ted, and I are in those chairs, and Eden and her mother are perched on higher stools at the corners. I'm not sure why we didn't pull the table away from the wall, but I'm a guest, so I'll eat where I'm told. Especially when I'm offered something this delicious. Ted was putting the big bowl of yellow rice, bright vegetables, and juicy seafood on the table when we arrived, so we started eating after Kerry gave me a quick tour of the apartment.

Checking through the colorful rice in my dish to make sure I'm not missing any shrimp or flaky pieces of fish, I ask Kerry the last time she saw Amanda Raines. Kerry had brought up the matter of the woman's death, which surprised Aiden, Eden, and me.

"The week before she died. Although after hearing what they found in her bloodstream, I'm beginning to wonder if that was what was wrong then."

Aiden and I quickly raise our heads. He

squints at Kerry and asks, "What do you mean? Was something wrong?"

Kerry is about the same size as Eden, just heavier in the hips and bosom. She has dark red hair, but it doesn't look artificially colored like her daughter's does, and it's not cut short and spiky. It's full and curly, and she has it pulled back with a headscarf. She's wearing a smock top she says she cooks in over a T-shirt and shorts. She picks up her glass of water, then looks out the front windows, thinking. Then she explains. "She was agitated. Amanda was normally high-strung, but not nervous-like. More determined and focused, which is why she was such a godsend for the Shrimp Festival when she came on the board a couple years ago."

Her face morphs into skepticism, and one eyebrow raises at me. "Eden says you met the festival's president, Victor Morrison, today. He's going to put in your air conditioning?"

"Yes. He seemed nice. Efficient..." I string out the last word because of her look.

"Oh, he's all that, I suppose," she says dismissively, shooting a quick look at her husband.

Ted stiffens in his seat beside me and plants his elbows on the table. "He shut us down! He acted like somehow our having a tattoo booth at the Shrimp Fest was disgusting."

"Dad!" Eden says, actually pushing him back into his seat from the height of her stool. "It's not him. It's the festival rules." She flips around to her other side. "Tell him, Aiden."

Aiden's mouth falls open, his eyebrows drop, and he shakes his head. "Not now. I want to go back to how Mrs. Raines was when you saw her." He turns to Eden's mother. "Did you know her well?"

"Well enough. We both frequented Naturally Good, you know, the health food store, and attended the seminars there." She waves a hand at her husband. "Ted can't sit through any kind of presentation on food or health, and as Amanda was also always alone, we sort of bonded." After a sigh her lips close together in sadness, and she looks down at her plate. "I'll miss her," she breathes.

Aiden tries again. "So you'd know if something was off with her?"

Kerry's chin lifts. "I'm very good at picking up on others' moods and feelings. Right, Ted?" When her husband doesn't look up, only shrugs, she turns to her daughter. "Right, Eden?"

"True." Egged on from across the table by

Aiden, she adds, "So, tell us what was different with Amanda when you saw her."

Her mother sniffs and crosses her arms. "Her face was flushed. She said her heart had been racing, so we went over her regimen, but there was absolutely nothing in her supplements or diet that could explain it." Acknowledging Aiden, who is getting ready to speak, she nods. "Yes. Of course she was going to see her doctor. While we both believe in taking as much control of our own health as possible, we're not stupid. We know having a good doctor we trust is also important. She said she had made an appointment to see him as soon as the festival was over."

She suddenly stands up. "I don't want to talk about that anymore. It's just too sad, but you can see why I'm positive Amanda did not take those kinds of stimulants they are saying they found. It isn't possible. Can I get anyone else a refill on their water?"

Ted holds up his glass. "Me. Aiden, will you pass the bread? I'm having one more slice, and then I've got to quit." He accepts the bread and turns to me. "So, Miss Jewel. You don't have even one little tattoo?"

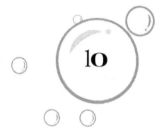

10

"I had a really good time at your parents' last night," I say as Eden comes around the corner into the kitchen. She's dressed for work while I'm still in a T-shirt and pajama shorts. We're both wearing a sheen of sweat as the house is sweltering already even though we just got up. "Sit down in front of the fan, and I'll fix you a cup of coffee."

"That air conditioning can't happen fast enough," she says as she sits. "It almost makes it worse spending time where it's cool and then coming back here, you know."

"I know. Believe me, I know! It made it very easy to be nice to Craig when we talked last night. Even though he was kind of incredulous that *I* was surprised he was dealing with the whole thing." With a quick look up at her, I say, "Don't worry. I'm not complaining. I did tell him thank you. Anyway, it seems like your parents really enjoy their apartment, huh?"

"It does, doesn't it? Smaller is better because Mom's never been one for cleaning and Daddy is not good at keeping anything up unless it has to do with his business. He loves that tattoo shop. Thanks," she says as I set a cup of coffee in front of her.

"He did seem pretty put out with Victor Morrison for not letting them have a booth at the Shrimp Festival."

"Yeah, sorry about that. He tends to go on and on about things." She rolls her eyes with a half grin, but her father did keep bringing it up.

"Well, now with the shop right downtown they shouldn't miss out on business, right? Even without a booth."

"Honestly, I think it was more about doing something different. Daddy likes to try new things. Kind of how Mom is with food and her vitamins. Oh yeah, and I had no idea she knew Amanda Raines."

"That was surprising, but then again, it does seem like everyone here knows everyone else. And it's crazy how quickly everyone heard about the blood tests." Leaning across the table I pick up the bottle of wine sitting there, still in its gift bag. "I wish I'd asked you about your folks before I brought this for them last night."

She laughs and gets up to walk to the refrigerator. "That's on me. How did I not realize you had a bottle of wine in that? I mean, what else could it be?" She stands with the door open. "But it's the thought that counts. Mom and Dad haven't had a drink in years. They quit when Mom got into the organic food and supplements." Coming back to the table with an apple, she sits down. "I think Mom felt Daddy was drinking too much, so she made a wholesale change." She laughs. "Daddy does whatever Mom thinks is best. So, what are you doing today?"

"Nothing here! I decided anything in this corner of hell can wait until we have air. I'm going to the beach. Taking my chair, my book, and a towel."

"Good for you. I'm jealous. Maybe I'll go down there this afternoon." As she walks back and forth, getting ready to leave, she picks up my book from the counter. "I do have to say Timothy Raines is attractive. Wikipedia said he's in his forties, but he doesn't even look that old. I always figured these author pictures on books were fixed up. Photoshopped."

"Is that why you kept hiding when he was here the other day?"

With a grin and a wrinkle of her nose, she turns to head out of the kitchen. She's out the door before I can stand and carry my coffee to the counter. Once there I lean onto my elbows, pick up the book, and look at the back.

"So. How about you and I take a trip to the beach, Mr. Raines?"

"They're going to arrest me! I just know they are!" are the frantic words I hear as I come out of the stairwell onto the narrow side deck at Lucy and her mother's place. I'd parked my car with my towel and book inside in the shade underneath their stilted beach house.

Before I could get out of my house and head for the beach, Lucy called, asking me to come over to help deal with a problem. Sounds like the problem is just around the corner.

"Hello?" I say as I step around the corner onto the full deck.

"There you are!" Lucy exclaims. She

jumps up from her seat under the umbrella, which is blocking the bright morning sun. She grabs my arm, but instead of pulling me forward toward the crying woman, she motions for me to lower my head to hers. When I'm there, she whispers, "That's Martha Morrison. She needs our help. I've called the others."

She pulls me to the table, and I duck under the umbrella to keep it from hitting me square in the face. The woman I heard earlier is seated there, rocking back and forth as she moans. She grabs the hem of my long shirt and jerks me closer as she looks up. "You have to help me. I didn't do it. I didn't kill Amanda. I was trying to *help* her!"

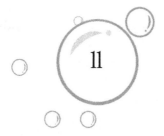

11

Lucy presses me into a seat, and then, holding her phone and saying she needs to make a call, she darts into the house. My knees are touching those of the crying woman, so I reach out to pat her leg, then pull back. Morrison? Could she be the wife of my air conditioning guy?

She reaches out and grabs my hand. "You're Mrs. Mantelle, aren't you? I've seen you around town, but I like to wait to be introduced to people. I've never picked up on that Southern thing of thinking everyone is my best friend. I'm embarrassed for you to see me like this." With her other hand she's dabbing at her eyes with a wadded-up tissue.

"Oh, that's okay. Yes, I'm Mrs. Mantelle. Call me Jewel." I chuckle and lean toward her. "I'm not from here either, so I completely understand what you're saying." She's around my age, but she looks stressed and older. Then again, she *is* talking about her friend she's just found out was murdered. Her gray hair is cut short and looks like the top is set on small curlers nightly. She's not wearing the mandatory makeup many of my new friends sport at all hours of the day, which is just as telling as her northern accent. Not northern as in New York or Boston or New Jersey, but still, it's from somewhere in that area. She's got to be Victor's wife. But like she said, we're not best friends, so I'm not asking.

"There's Lucy!" I jump out of the seat as Lucy comes barreling back out onto the porch.

"I had to call and check in with the office. Sit back down, Jewel. I'll sit here." She pauses. "Or should we go in? Mother's here. Maybe she can help?"

"Birdie?" Martha asks. "Oh, no, I'm so embarrassed. Calling you like this and letting you call your friends. Maybe I'm overreacting. I so hate to think what your mother will think. She hears enough of my moaning in Sunday school." She sniffles but doesn't start crying again. "What *was* I thinking?"

Lucy waves her hands. "Balderdash! This is what friends are for. Mother loves you. Mother loves everyone. Let's go inside." She pulls open the door and motions us in. "I'll put on some coffee."

It takes a while, but we all have coffee, all of us being Lucy, her mother, Martha, Tamela, Annie, and me. Cherry is back in Atlanta for a family wedding this weekend, so we'll have to fill her in later.

Annie arrived with a Danish ring in an aluminum pan from the grocery store as she'd been shopping when Lucy called her. Tamela arrived in workout clothes after excusing herself from yoga with her husband, one of the latest activities Hert is trying in his retirement.

Tamela fans herself by pulling in and out on her long T-shirt. "I thought Hert would be over yoga by now and I could enjoy the sessions by myself. He might actually last longer at it than I do."

Martha shakes her head. "Oh no, Tamela. You must keep going. Your husband too. Don't be a quitter like me." She takes a breath, and her voice weakens. "I used to love yoga."

Annie grunts, a piece of pastry almost to her mouth. "Yoga, huh? Maybe I should look into that. I've heard that's not like real exercise. I'm not fond of sweating."

Martha's eyes flash and Tamela's roll. Lucy lifts her hand at Annie. "Ignore her, Martha. We're here to help you. So, tell us what's going on."

With another stab of her dark eyes at Annie, Martha takes a deep breath. "Yes, I believe in the merits of yoga, but also in eating as organically as possible. As Amanda and I shared this belief, this is a good place to start. You see, Amanda and I exchanged recipes quite often."

I blurt out, "Do you know Kerry Church?"

Martha's nostrils actually flare but only for a moment. Then she pushes her wadded-up tissue to her nose. "I believe so. Red hair? Tattoos?"

"I guess. I didn't notice her having tattoos, but she probably does." Across from me I notice that Annie caught the nose flare at the mention of Eden's mother. Annie's a bit defensive of the girl she hopes to call her daughter-in-law one day. She snaps a quick look at me, letting me know she picked up on something but is going to behave, so I rush on. "It's just that she mentioned the same kind of thing about Amanda. Health food and supplements."

"Supplements?" Lucy asks. "Isn't that what you were talking about when you got here, Martha?" She takes one of Martha's hands and pulls it toward her, directing the woman's attention away from the rest of us, our interruptions and lack of focus. "What were you saying?"

Lucy's soft voice and drawl work like lotion, soothing Martha's drawn face. Lucy leans toward her, and it's like they're the only two in the room as Martha Morrison starts telling her story.

"Those supplements they are saying caused Amanda's heart attack are not that uncommon. But she didn't use them. She was very careful. Very careful." Martha pauses and looks down at her hand laying in Lucy's. "I was careful too. I know I never mixed things up. Never!" Loudly she says, "It's impossible. Just impossible!"

She startles the rest of us with this, and we look at each other with widened eyes. Lucy, however, just strokes Martha's hand and waits. Finally she whispers, "What was there to mix up?"

Martha lifts her head but only stares at

Lucy, blinking but not talking. Suddenly she
stands. "I shouldn't have come here." Lucy
tries to keep their hands connected by also
standing, but Martha pulls away. Looking
around at the rest of us, she gives a little cry.
"What was I thinking?" Grabbing her purse
from the floor beside her, she turns toward
the doors to the deck and rushes outside.

Lucy follows her out but comes back in
less than a minute. "She says she'll call me
later. I can tell you what she told me before
y'all got here, but I was hoping we could all
work together. She said she wanted our help
to figure it out, that she was very confused. I
suggested calling y'all, and she was all for it.
Sorry. Can I get anyone anything before I sit
back down?"

Annie speaks up. "No…" she draws out,
looking past us at the beach. Then she clicks
her tongue. "I bet I know what she all of a
sudden realized she didn't want to tell us."
She looks around and grins, her red lipstick
only barely smudged from the pastry. "Ol'
Victor is having some trouble in the bedroom!"

Birdie groans and shakes her head. That's
the first sound she's made since we came inside. Lucy said she's sulking and to ignore
her.

The rest of us stop in our tracks, mouths dropped at Annie's conjecture.

Tamela sputters. "What in the world? Where did you come up with that?"

Annie arches an eyebrow. "I wanted to see what Mrs. Morrison had to say first, so I didn't mention that I have a list of what all they found in Amanda's bloodstream or that I was up googling them practically all night. Some are just out-and-out energy enhancers, but some were for male libido enhancement." She shakes her head. "Poor old Victor." She blasts out a laugh. "Poor old Martha!"

Lucy chews on her lip as she nods. "I can think of three different ways, all illegal I'm pretty sure, you might've gotten your hands on that list, so I'm not even going to ask, but what you're saying sounds about right. Martha said she'd never mixed things up. Before y'all got here she was telling me in an offhand way that she'd added some things for Victor's health into muffins and such for him for the last few months as the festival really got going. Then she said she also made muffins for Amanda, but she'd never mixed things up." Lucy sighs as she folds her arms and rests one knee on the hassock in front of her. "She just kept saying that. Saying that she didn't mix things up."

"But she can't be the only person that has these types of supplements," Tamela says, sinking back into her seat on the couch. "Why does she think anyone would suspect her? Maybe she mixed the muffins up by mistake?"

With only the sound of the waves crashing on the beach outside, we all look around, silently going over what this strange meeting with Martha Morrison was about. Then Annie leans forward, bracelets rattling, her bright eyes lit up. "Maybe she did mix things up. But maybe she mixed things up on purpose."

At the same time Tamela and I ask, "Why?"

After another pause Annie squints and cocks her head. "What if Amanda Raines was getting the benefit of all that baking Martha was doing? What if Victor had too much newfound vigor for just one bedroom and Martha wanted to weed out the competition?"

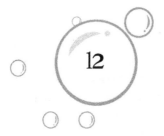

12

"I hear you're getting air conditioning," Annie says as she steps into the space underneath Lucy's house, where our cars are parked.

I'm still on the stairs, but her words stop me. "Yes. From Victor Morrison's company. How awkward is that?"

"Awkward or perfect for investigating?" Tamela says with a poke in my back. "Go on. I've got to get home and get changed for bunco. Thank the Lord it's all women so Hert can't join. I have to have some time without him."

"Have fun. I'm heading to the beach to finish that Timothy Raines book." I let Tamela pass Annie and me. "Lucy said I can just leave my car here as long as she can get out." Waving to Tamela as she prepares to back out onto A1A, I turn to Annie. "You're welcome to join me, but I'm not talking. I'm reading."

"Not today. I'm watching the kids for Leesa and Adam this afternoon until Sunday. It's their anniversary, so they're going up to Savannah for the weekend." She opens her car door. "Come eat dinner with us tomorrow night. Leesa is leaving stuff for us to have a taco night. Tonight we're going to Chick-fil-A."

"I don't want to interfere with your grandkid time."

"Believe me, you're not interfering. I'd appreciate a hand. Taco night." She rolls her eyes. "Leesa works so hard to impress on me what a good mother she is that she always comes up with fun things for me to cook with the kids." She puts air quotes around the word "fun" and rolls her big, blue eyes. "My idea of fun is ordering pizza. Adam always raves about my home cooking, but what he doesn't get is that there weren't all these restaurants on Sophia Island when he was little. Of course, if there had been, it wouldn't've mattered. We were broke!"

"If you really want a hand, I'd love to come. The kids are cute." While she was talking, I got my beach bag and chair out of the car and slid my sunglasses on. "What time should I come over?"

"Five is good, or come earlier to swim if you want. You still have Leesa and Adam's address?"

"Yep. I'll call you in the morning. Maybe I will come to swim." She's getting in her car as I say bye and walk out the back of the parking area to stand underneath the deck. Lucy was heading to work and Birdie was ready for a nap, so I knew neither of them were up there.

I follow the sidewalk to a wooden walkover that allows people to cross the dunes without damaging them. From the high point of the crossover, I can see along the dune and the backs of the houses along the beach. There's a wide mix of housing on Sophia Island, and the beachfront is no different. Small, older homes. Small, newer homes. Modern, traditional, big, bigger, biggest, and those using every square inch of their property allowed. Including vertically. Property on Sophia Island isn't permitted to be taller than forty feet, but some homeowners have gotten around that rule by allowing their elevator shaft to rise above the limit. They say that's not actually the building, and this being Sophia, there's of course lots of discussion about it.

As I turn away from the houses, it's ocean as far as I can see. To my left there's more of a crowd near Main Beach, where there's parking and restaurants and a mini golf course. Along this stretch, however, there are only a few umbrellas and solitary people like me enjoying the last Friday in May on the beach.

The walkway slants down and the sawgrass sways in the ocean breeze as I walk through it and onto the open beach. I claim a spot, set my bag down, and open my chair. I apply a good helping of sunscreen and get settled.

Now, back to getting my hero out of the dire spot I left him in.

~~~~~~~

"So, is it good?" a man's voice asks from beside my chair.

I look up, straight into the sun. "Yes, it is." Pulling the bill of my hat down a bit, I laugh. "Oh, it's you." I close the book and hold it up. "It's yours."

"Oh, then I wholeheartedly approve. May I join you?" Timothy Raines asks as he reaches for the towel sticking out of my bag. He unrolls it and sits on it in the sand.

"Um, uh, sure." This is messing with the image I have of my hero, this getting my towel sandy.

"Do you like it?" he asks, his smile wide as he stares up at me through his sunglasses. His hair is tousled from the wind, and it might look even better than it did when it was all in place. His tan arms rest on his tan knees. He has on long shorts, a short-sleeve, dark green shirt, and leather flip-flops. So what's a little sand on my towel?

"I love it. How did you write this? It's not what I would ever have chosen to read, but it completely drew me in. As a matter of fact I just finished it, and I'm practically heartbroken that it's done."

He winks. "Don't worry. There are more." He shifts and reaches into his pocket. "Want me to sign it to you?" he asks, and I gladly hand the book over.

As he turns to the title page and writes an inscription, I look around. "Were you just down here walking?"

"No. I was looking for you."

He can have the towel. "You were looking for me?" Okay, why is my voice so squeaky?

He closes the book and hands it to me. "Tamela told me where to find you. I called her because I need to get back into your house." A frown pulls at his face, and he takes off his glasses to rub his eyes. "I can't think in my mother's house. All I can see is everything I need to do. Where do I even start with cleaning it out? Plus, I get so angry thinking she should still be here, but I have a deadline to get my synopsis to my publisher. That absolutely cannot wait."

"Well, of course. Feel free to come by whenever you need to. Speaking of your mother, have you found anything else out?"

"No word on being able to have a funeral. As for who is responsible, well, we'll see." He stands in one fluid motion, and I find myself looking up into the sun again.

He picks up my towel and shakes it behind us. As he folds it back up he says, "Can I come by later?" He stuffs my towel back into my bag and leans closer to my chair and my upturned face. "Tonight maybe? Bring a bottle of wine?" he suggests.

When I manage to nod, he squeezes my bare shoulder, turns, and walks away.

The beach sure is toasty today.

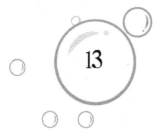

13

"How are you feeling, though?" I ask my daughter Erin again. I needed to make some phone calls, so I decided to do them from the air-conditioned comfort of my car in a shaded parking spot downtown.

Erin picked up my call and began a litany of reasons why I shouldn't proceed down the path to divorce and instead should just wait things out. I've agreed with her several times, which hasn't kept her from repeating herself anyway. She also refuses to talk about herself, which is making me uneasy.

"Seriously. What is going on with you and the baby? Your dad and I are fine. He's even getting air conditioning put in the house. We're not in any hurry to do anything."

There's silence, and then she clears her

throat. "The doctor wants me to rest more. Thinks that could help with my nausea and, well, my blood pressure."

"Your blood pressure is high? How high?"

"I didn't tell you when we were there because I didn't want everyone to worry."

I grit my teeth. Erin hates to be the center of attention; she always has. "Honey, there are times when people need to worry. What exactly did the doctor say? When did you see her?"

"This morning. She wants me to rest, put my feet up more, and that's what I'm doing. Work has already been great, so there won't be a problem. I'm cutting back my hours, and I already mostly work from home, so it's all good. I no longer have to go into the office at all."

"Do you want me to come out there and help?"

"No, Mom. Wait until the baby comes. I'm really fine. Just worried about you and Dad."

"Well, stop that right now. Don't give us a second thought."

"Okay, I promise."

She sounds better than she did when I first called, so I tell her about the book I just read and about meeting the author. That he's coming over tonight because he's setting his next book in our house. We end with her laughing about me having dinner over a tattoo parlor. She's the worrier of my kids. The boys are still too young to really concern themselves with anyone else, although Chris has reached out several times via text this week. He's finishing his junior year and is trying to make a decision about grad school. We've mostly texted about that decision, but he's also asked about me, which is nice. Drew is in the middle of baseball season, so he might as well not exist right now. Sadie has never had time to chat, so it's no surprise that my only communication with her has been a couple of pictures of Carver. She only deals in what is actually happening. She doesn't waste time with what-if's and maybe's.

But her sister? Her sister is all over what *might* happen. She's my worrier, and now she's going to have a baby to worry over. Poor thing.

I turn off the car and get out. I called in an order of spicy Thai noodles from Café Mango to take home and eat as a late lunch. A full order makes a couple of meals, and since they are served cold, there's not even any reheating to do.

Café Mango is on the corner of Third

Street, and along with a brewpub has two lush garden areas to eat in. I've got to get more used to eating out alone, but it feels so weird. I'd rather just carry my meal home. The side garden area I have to walk through to get inside is busy, but it's an after-lunch kind of busy. No hurry. People are enjoying glasses of wine and looking sated and relaxed. The waitstaff are taking the time to chat with their customers, and there's laughter interspersed with the talk, the breeze, and the clinking of dishes. This living in a vacation town takes some getting used to.

But I'm having fun working on that.

"I have an order to pick up. Mantelle," I say to the young woman behind the inside counter. She turns and reads the names on several tickets attached to bags behind her.

"Here it is," she says brightly. She turns to the computer as she sits my bag in front of me.

"Jewel," I hear behind me.

"Charlie!" I turn to find Aiden's partner, Officer Greyson, whom I haven't seen in lately. Then again, not having the police visit your house is probably a good thing. "Have you finished lunch?" I ask hopefully. Maybe I won't have to go home and eat alone. "The garden looks so nice."

"It is nice, but yes, I've eaten. How have you been?" He's off duty apparently, as he's wearing a loose-fitting cotton shirt and shorts, and it makes him even easier to talk to. Although we've never had trouble talking. My friends enjoy ribbing me about Charlie's attention, and as my smile grows I realize how much I enjoy chatting with him.

"I'm fine." I pull my hand through my hair. "I've been on the beach all morning. Such a beautiful day. Oh, yes," I say as the cashier tells me how much I owe. I turn to her but keep talking to Charlie. "How are you doing? Looks like you're also having a relaxing day. You're off today?" I ask as I sign my receipt. "We've missed seeing you around." I pick up my bag and turn back with a wide smile.

"Jewel, this is my wife, Fiona."

Well, that's the shock of the day, and I've already had a pretty full morning. I work to keep my wide smile pasted on. I should be happy to finally be meeting my friend's other half, I remind myself.

"Julie? What a cute name," the blonde woman purrs as she holds her hand out to me. "Fiona Greyson." We barely touch hands before she pulls away, the corners of her lips turning down. "Charles, I'll see you at home," she says, breezing behind him toward the door.

"Oh. What a pretty name. Fiona. Well, I'll let you go," I say to her back. Then I look at the floor because my face is heating up, though I can't imagine why. I just want to go home, but Charlie's between me and the door.

He touches my elbow. "Can I ask you something? Here, let's step outside." He moves ahead to the door, and I follow. I fumble in my purse to find my sunglasses and put them on.

"There," he says. "Little more room out here." We move to stand beside the sidewalk and the bushes. "So, you've met that author guy, Tim Raines, right?"

"Yes. Why?"

"What did you think about him?"

I finally look up at Charlie. "He's fine, I guess. Listen, I need to get home. My lunch, you know." I hold up my bag like there's something getting cold in it, even though I know the noodles are just fine.

"Oh, sure. Okay. Um, listen. Uh…"

My face is heating up again. I blurt, "It's fine. Your wife, I mean. It was nice to meet her. Fiona. She seems nice."

He pauses and looks down the sidewalk, a

muscle in his jaw jumping. "Oh, yeah. Okay, anyway, I should probably go, too, seeing as this Raines thing is now officially a *murder investigation*. But, whatever, enjoy your lunch." He turns abruptly and stalks away, ignoring my dropped-open mouth.

And they say getting takeout is easy.

"Yes, I'm sure. He said it's officially a murder investigation." I have Annie on speakerphone as I drive home, so I have to listen to her playing Twister with her grandkids while she's talking to me.

"A.J., get off my leg!" she shrieks just before there's more screaming and laughter. "Go watch TV, I need to talk to Miss Jewel," she yells, then in a lower voice says, "Dang. I hate to lose, even to my grandkids."

"Sounds like they weren't playing fair."

"Hey, that's right. A.J. cheated by climbing on me, so I didn't actually lose. Let me go outside."

I wait for her as I drive across Centre Street. The sidewalks are full of shoppers enjoying the sunny afternoon. I turn a corner and enter the shady, peaceful area of downtown near our house.

Annie says, "Whew," and I imagine she's

just sat down beside the pool. "It's hot out here," she says. "How was the beach?"

"Nice. I'll tell you who I saw there in a minute."

"Silly girl. Of course I know that Mr. Good-Looking Author was looking for you. But where did you talk to Charlie?"

"At Café Mango. I was picking up lunch, and he was there with his wife. Anyway, he—"

"You met Fiona! Isn't she a fright?"

"A fright? She's very pretty, maybe a little cold, but nothing I'd call 'a fright.'"

"Well, believe me, she's a fright; you just have to get to know her. Why he's still with her, nobody knows, but what about Amanda being murdered? Maybe we should've been more scared to be with Martha Morrison this morning."

I pull into our yard and up the drive. "Yeah. Maybe. But listen, I've got to go." I hang up before she can say anything else. After all, that is Martha Morrison's husband standing there waiting on me.

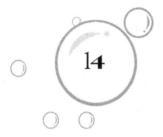

14

"Hey, Mrs. Mantelle. So you went to the beach this morning, I hear. Nice day for it." Victor meets me and opens my car door as soon as I roll to a stop. "Anything I can carry in for you?"

"No, I'm leaving my chair in the trunk. Thanks, though." I get out, and he slams the door behind me. "So, how did you hear I was at the beach?" Does he know his wife was at Lucy's? Does he know what she was talking about? I keep walking so I don't have to look at him.

He follows me up the steps. "That young woman, Eden. I stopped for a coffee and she told me. Were you down there by yourself?"

"Yes. Doing some reading." At the front door I stop and hold up my bag from Café

Mango. "I picked up lunch. Is there something I can help you with? I'm kind of starving." I laugh, and he does too.

With his hands on his hips, he announces, "Just that I drew up your estimate and got it out to your husband first thing. I also emailed a copy to you. He wants to get started right away." He smiles at me and then lifts an eyebrow. "If it's okay with you."

"Of course. As soon as possible. Everything is good with the historic people?"

He inhales, and his chest expands. "Sure is. They trust me and know I'll not let 'em down. So then I'll get right on it!" He starts down the steps but yells over his shoulder, "You just leave everything to me. I'll take care of it all." Climbing in his truck, he says, "I'll be back in a bit. You'll still be here?"

"For the rest of the day."

He salutes me, and then he's off, pulling around my car and bouncing through the gate with barely a pause at the road.

I unlock the front door and push into the house. The heat is unbearable, and I decide that even before I eat I'm texting Craig to tell him thank you.

"Well, of course I meant to move in. What did you think I meant?"

Timothy Raines stands on my front porch with the bottle of wine as promised. But he also has a suitcase at his feet and a garment bag thrown over his shoulder—not as promised.

"I thought you just wanted to hang out here and get out of your mother's house for a bit," I answer, but I'm frozen in the doorway, so he remains on the porch. Why would he think he could move in here? "We don't even have air conditioning."

He hands me the bottle of wine and then picks up his suitcase. "Oh, that's not a problem," he says as he advances toward me. I automatically move back. "I'm a very easy guest." He relieves himself of his bags and turns to me, taking the bottle of wine back. "Let's get this open so we can have a drink while you show me my room." From the kitchen he adds loudly, "No fuss at all. Just a bed and a desk are all I require, although I can write just as well at this table. Here's a corkscrew!"

"But you can't stay here."

He's found two glasses and pours the red wine. "Only for a little while. I just can't think at my mother's house." He looks up at me. "I told you that, right?" I nod and open my mouth, but before I can say anything, he's moved on. "I need to soak in the ambiance here, and you can't possibly be using all these rooms. Tamela told me your whole family was just here." He hands me my glass and then clinks the edge of it with his. "You won't even know I'm here."

He moves into the living room and sets his glass down beside my big chaise lounge, right where the fan is aimed. Then he takes his seat. *My* seat. "This is such a comfortable chair." He settles back, lifts his glass, and takes a sip. "Jewel, sit. Let's talk."

I guess there's no need to kick him out right away. I might as well enjoy the wine and relax a bit. But first I put the fan on oscillate and position myself so that I can also enjoy the breeze. "I did enjoy your book," I say. "I finished it on the beach. How do you do that? Come up with such a crazy story, with terrorists and everything?"

"It just came in dribs and drabs, and then once the story got going, it was work to keep up." He looks around. "This book, though, it's different. It's more of a family story. Don't you just love old houses and thinking of all the stories that have been lived out in them?"

I shudder. "Not especially. But then maybe it's because I'm living in one now."

"I take it your husband, even though it would be *his* family's stories, is just as ambivalent?"

"I guess. We haven't really talked about it."

We sit in the quiet, watch the fan turn, and sip our wine. Tim has on dark shorts and a graphic T-shirt, which looks new. He seems so at home here—not just on Sophia Island but here, in my house. Craig never looked that at home in our living room.

"Will your husband be home this weekend?" he asks.

I jump. It's like he read my mind. "No. I mean, he was just here for the holiday weekend."

"That's true. So you can just give me the room he stayed in." He looks away from me, closes his eyes, and lifts his face to the breeze. "You do have separate rooms these days, I assume."

"Why would you assume that?" Did I tell Tamela we slept apart? I can't remember, but it had to have come from her.

With his eyes still closed he answers. "Because you look and act like a single woman. I'm a writer. I pay attention to people. Especially people that interest me…" He lets that drag out, then shifts his focus to me, eyes open and piercing. "For the story. You interest me for the story."

I swallow. "The story?"

He shifts forward in the chaise. "Please let me stay here, Jewel. I know I should've asked, but I was afraid you'd say no. I need to be here for just a couple of days. Clear my head from what happened to my mother and soak in this place. Please." He smiles. "It really will help."

"Well, okay. Sure. For a couple of days. You just caught me off guard." I look up the stairs. "Of course there's plenty of space."

He slides to the very end of his seat and grabs my hand. "And the book will be magnificent."

I pull away. He went from sincere to intense in the space of a couple of seconds. I stand up. "Let me see where I can put you. Oh wait." I pass the staircase and walk toward the back door. Turning to the right, I enter the room Erin and Paul stayed in. "This room is all made up, and there's even a small table and chair."

From nowhere near me he exclaims, "Just look at this desk. This is perfect!" He's doing his exclaiming from Craig's office. He must have opened the closed door, which I've been ignoring.

"No. I don't think so. My husband's stuff is in there." I follow his voice and find him in Craig's chair pulled up to Craig's desk. But… where is Craig's stuff? The desktop is clean. I try to remember what was on the shelf or the desk, but it was always just work papers and computer cords and, well, stuff.

There's nothing there now. Craig has moved out.

"I'll sleep across the hall and work in here. It's perfect!" Tim spins the desk chair to face me. "Jewel, it's like it was meant to be, isn't it?"

My stomach does a slow roll, and I swallow to keep it still. I turn back into the hall shaking my head, trying to take a deep breath, and working to stop my heart from pounding.

Craig moved out.

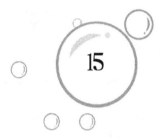

15

Car doors slamming wake me to a sunlit room. Early sun, but still, it's finally morning. Every other time I woke throughout the night, it was pitch black.

Finally. I can get up.

My relief subsides when I hear the voices that apparently go with the car doors. I fling off the damp sheet and get out of bed, reaching for the robe I laid out last night. I mean, I do have Mr. Raines living in the house now. I hope all the noise hasn't woken him.

Dashing out the bedroom door, down the hall, and then the staircase, I jolt to a stop at the bottom. Timothy is awake and has even managed to open the front door, where Victor Morrison stands.

"Hope we didn't get here too early," the

older man says, staring at my guest. He drops his eyes to the paperwork in his hand, then sticks it out. "Here."

I rush up and grab the papers. "Thanks for getting the door, Mr. Raines. You can go back to bed—oh! Or whatever you were doing." From this vantage point I can see past Mr. Morrison to his crew standing at the bottom of the front steps. There are a lot of grins down there, so I ignore them and look at their boss. "Mr. Raines is a guest here—I mean, in his own room, of course!"

That line from Shakespeare floats into my head—"Methinks the lady doth protest too much"—so I shut up. Then I turn and see the biggest grin of all on my houseguest's face. He raises his eyebrows at me and says, "Think I will go back to bed." He turns, but adds loudly, "As you suggested."

Victor is directing his men on which supplies to gather, so I address his back. "You're ready to begin work?"

"Oh, yes, ma'am!" He spins back to me, and all traces of a grin are gone. He's all business. "Finished up measuring yesterday afternoon. Those papers are the copy of the contract I promised you, same as your husband signed. There's also the informational pamphlets on the system and a tentative work schedule. We'll try to stay out of your way and, uh, the way of your guest." He swallows, and I can tell how much effort it's taking for him to not smile suggestively or wink. He obviously finds this highly entertaining, a strange man in my house when he knows my husband is out of town.

It's not helping that I'm sweating and my cheeks are hot. I can't think of what to say, so I nod, step back, and shrug at him. "Okay. Sure."

A bit of a smirk slips out as he turns away, but I ignore it, close the door, and march back to the stairs. I dart up them after a peek to see that Timothy's door is shut. At the top of the stairs, I stop at Eden's door. It's also shut, but it's Saturday, so she should've been at work a while ago. Or could she be off to-day? I stride down the hall. I'll get dressed and then see if she's still here.

A cool shower helps with my foggy brain and flushed body. My morning is free, but I can't settle on what to do. Every idea comes back around to wondering what Timothy is doing. Finally, before I can start sweating too much, I pull open my door and see a note from Eden taped to the banister: "Call Me!" Her door is still closed. I wonder if this note was here earlier? It could've been. It was still pretty dark up here, and I was in a hurry both leaving the room and returning to it.

"Hi," I say into the phone as I descend the stairs. "You wanted me to call?"

"Whose car was that at the house all night? Maybe it's none of my business, but it kind of is, isn't it? I mean I live there, too, and well, I just think I should know. Don't you? Unless it's none of my business! But, well…" The torrent finally dribbles to stop.

"Mr. Raines is renting the downstairs rooms to write in."

There's no response, and I can practically hear her eyelashes fluttering as she thinks that through. Then she asks in a whisper, "Tim Raines? The author guy? Why?"

"Because…" Now I'm whispering as I sneak around downstairs looking for our guest. "Because he wants to be in the house because of the book. You know—the book."

"Oh. The book. Okay, well. I've got to get back to work."

"Okay. Hey, they've started on the air conditioning."

She squeals. "Yes! Gotta go."

A low voice comes from the living room. "Guess I should've parked my car around back."

"Oh! You scared me. Where are you?"

"Here," he says from beside the huge fire-place. "This little alcove. What do you think it could've been for?" he asks as he steps out of the hidden nook and looks at it.

"I've never thought about it. A bookcase maybe?"

The fireplace is big and sticks out of the wall, forming a wide, deep mantel of stone. There's a foot-high hearth that needs to be cleaned of all the years of soot and dust that are embedded in it, which makes the whole area dark and easy to ignore. And then there's the little nook Mr. Raines was standing in, inset behind the fireplace and to one side, not really hidden, but not open to the room.

"How would a bookcase work in here?" he asks, stepping into the nook again. "It's too deep for one on the back wall and too narrow for them on the side walls. Plus it's very dark."

I shrug and step away from the odd little cubbyhole I'd never really thought about.

He follows me. "So, my car has piqued interest in the locals?"

"No. Have you had coffee?" I ask as I enter the kitchen with him close behind.

"Yes, thank you, I have. But, Jewel, you're not being honest. Your little friend on the phone and that contractor were both very interested." He leans on the counter beside me and folds his arms. He's wearing shorts and an old T-shirt, but he smells clean, and I notice his hair is wet.

"Did you take a shower?"

"Yes. Rather inconvenient to not have one down on this floor, but when I went upstairs I could hear your hair dryer, so I just went on and used the hall bathroom before asking permission." He smiles and spikes an eyebrow. "No harm, no foul." He pulls out a chair for me to sit down. "So back to the matter at hand. Your reputation."

"My reputation?" I choke on the words and set my coffee down without tasting it.

He laughs out loud. "I'm joking, I'm joking. Your discomfort was just too good to ignore. Your contractor was being egged on by his men, and your friend on the phone—Eden, I believe—is a tad nosy, which I find admirable since, as an author, I'm usually the nosiest person around." He leans back in his chair and stares at me.

It feels like he's baiting me with the shower and reputation talk, so I decide to not engage. After a long sip of coffee, I set my mug down again and pick up the papers Mr. Morrison gave me earlier. I'd left them here on the table when I went upstairs. "Victor has laid out a pretty tight schedule for himself and his crew."

Timothy juts forward. "Victor?" He pulls the papers so he can see them, then takes them from my hands.

"Hey, give me those," I demand and grab them back.

He doesn't fight me, just settles back, concentrating on the doorway leading to the living room. "That was Victor Morrison." After a pause he sighs. "Of course."

"Yes. Do you know him?"

"I've heard of him. That wasn't exactly how I pictured him." He stands. "I need to get to work," he says, and he walks through the kitchen toward the back hallway. The last thing I hear is his office door closing. No—Craig's office door. No... whatever.

Only a couple of minutes of reading is all it takes for me to know I don't really want to know how the air conditioning system will work. It's called a retrofit system, which requires no large ductwork and is perfect for an older house. The price tag is a little over ten thousand dollars, and while that's a lot of money, it will certainly be worth it. Craig told me he'd taken out a home equity loan to pay for this and other renovations when I freaked out about the cost. I stack all the papers together with the schedule on top. Looks like they'll be here every day this week.

I pick up my phone. Wonder if anyone's heard anything else about Tim's mother's murder? Cherry is still out of town, and Annie is busy with her grandkids. Lucy is playing in a tennis tournament this morning—also organizing it, I think—so I'll leave her alone. Tamela and I chatted yesterday and agreed to keep each other in the loop if we heard anything, so I guess the answer is no. Even though I put my phone back on the table, I quickly pick it up and dial Craig before I can talk myself out of it.

He answers immediately. "Hey. Morrison is there working, right? Is there a problem?"

"Good morning to you too. No problem. Just thought I'd check in with you. How are things down there?"

"Fine, fine. Is that work schedule okay for you? I know you usually have plans with your friends there." Snideness creeps into his voice. "Hope it won't mess any of your fun up."

This call might not have been a good idea. I take a breath. "No. It looks fine. I, uh, I really appreciate you taking care of everything. I looked over the information, and I think it's perfect. I'd never heard of a system like that."

He chuckles. "Honestly, I hadn't either until I started doing some research. The price is steep, but it looks like the best deal in the long run." He pauses and then sighs. "After Memorial Day weekend I felt bad I hadn't looked into it before. I'm really sorry you're stuck there with the heat and the renovation work."

"Oh! Oh, well, don't even think about all that stuff. We make a good team!" I catch myself too late. We often said that line because it was true. Now it just feels empty. And awkward.

The line is silent. Then he clears his throat and says, "I guess it's still true—in some ways. But listen, I've got to go."

"Working on Saturday?"

"No. Um, I'm going sailing."

"Sailing? Where?"

"Here. A guy here owns a boat, and some of us are going out for the day. They want to get going, so I'll let you go. Call if you need anything, but Morrison seems to have a good handle on things."

He's gone before I can say "okay" or "goodbye" or anything.

"Sailing, huh?" Timothy says from behind me. "That'll be fun."

Grinding my teeth, I rise from my chair

and face him. "Do you always listen to other people's conversations?"

"Yes. Everyone does. I'm honest, though, and I admit it. Plus, you have your volume turned up awfully loud. Might as well be on speakerphone." He puts his coffee cup under the spigot. "Listen, I'll bring over some coffee pods from my mother's so I don't use up all of yours. She didn't drink it, but she kept a stash for me and a small, one-cup machine."

I look through the refrigerator. I can't believe Craig is going sailing. He told the kids it was fun down there, but I thought he was just making that up. Sure, we make a good team. He's off sailing, and I've got an eavesdropping author and a crew of workmen tearing up my house.

"Whoa! What did that refrigerator do to you?" the eavesdropper asks when I slam the door.

"I'm going out."

"Are you bringing back breakfast?"

I ignore him and stomp up the stairs, but I'm barely to the top before I realize there really isn't much food in the house. I haven't restocked since the holiday weekend. I lean over the top banister and yell, "Timothy!"

He saunters out of the kitchen, coffee in hand, and looks up at me. "Yes?"

"I'm going to the store. I don't know how you envision this arrangement, but I'm not cooking for you."

"I'd never dream of it," he declares, but the way his eyebrows flatten and his mouth puckers, I think he's making fun of me. I straighten up and don't look down at him.

"Eden brings her own food. If you make a list of a few things you'd like and leave the money to pay for them, I'll pick them up."

"Deal!" he says and swirls around to go back into the kitchen, yelling, "I'll leave a short list on the counter. Do you want a check or cash later?"

Of course. I roll my eyes and shout, "Cash later, I guess."

I catch myself before I slam my bedroom door, but I growl loudly and spit out, "Sailing!"

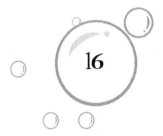

16

"It's so still out there," I say as I shut the back door to the house and pass the cracked-open office door. Getting a peek over my shoulder, I see Timothy isn't seated at the desk as I had assumed. The kitchen is also empty. "Great. Of course he's not here to help carry in groceries."

Another two loads and the car is empty, the counters full. I'm really sweating now, and there's still no houseguest in sight. His car hasn't been moved, so I assume he hasn't gone far. Then I hear footsteps and step into the living room to see him sauntering down the staircase.

"Jewel. You're home."

"What are you doing up there?"

"Snooping around," he says as he breezes past me and starts looking in the grocery bags. "How was shopping?"

"Fine. What were you looking around at up there?"

"Just the house. Remember why I'm here? I'm writing a book set in this house. I need to get a feel for it. Plus, the workmen are in the attic." He winks at me over his shoulder. "I thought I'd better keep an eye on them for you. Kind of like the man of the house."

"Stop digging through my groceries." I swipe at him, as he's pulling things out and setting them wherever he feels so inclined. "Those are your bags over there."

"Miss Jewel?" comes from the living room, and a young man sticks his head around the doorway.

"Yes, Hector?"

"Mr. Morrison has some questions for you up on the second floor. Can you come up?"

"Sure. Let me put a couple of things in the freezer, and then I'll be right there."

Hector vanishes, and I look through the bags Timothy was just disturbing. "I *did* have all the cold stuff together."

"Here, let me help," Timothy says as he comes up beside me and starts reaching past me and around me.

He's a bit taller I am, and I'm hemmed into the corner by his body. I bump him back with my shoulder, but he just looks down at me. He's not moved at all by my bumping, sighing, or my glare.

"Jewel. Really?" He presses even farther against me and leans down but suddenly backs away. "Just trying to help."

Clutching the carton of ice cream and a bag of frozen vegetables, I turn to the refrigerator and shove the items into the freezer. Then I dart past him and out of the room.

In the living room, I steady myself with a hand on the back of the couch.

I honestly thought for a minute that he was going to kiss me! Shaking my head, I dash up the stairs.

That's just crazy.

"Pardon my French, Mrs. Mantelle," Victor Morrison says when he realizes I'm standing just inside the door and heard everything he said to his two workmen. He touches my elbow and steers me out the door.

"No problem. Is everything okay?"

"Of course. I'm just under a lot of pressure to get this job done. Can't stand thinking of you roasting alive in this place one moment longer than necessary." In the hallway, he stops. Then, with a glance back to where he was working, he shakes his head. "I have trouble explaining to my young crews how critical our work is. If a family is uncomfortable in their home, it's hard for them to be happy in their home." He pulls his eyes away from me, and the muscles in his jaw work back and forth, keeping his lips tightly closed. He swallows, sniffs, then gives me a smile through watery eyes. "Folks having a happy home is the most important thing to me." He clears his throat and steps past me. "Look there, in the bathroom."

We enter the room, and he points out the subtle way the small, circular vents are coming out of the wall. "You can see they'll be hardly noticeable when the fixture is painted to match the wall."

"Oh my! You're right." I raise my hand toward it. "But it's not hooked up now, is it?"

He laughs and folds his arms over his thick chest. "No, ma'am. Not yet, but it won't be long. I'm pushing my guys for you..." He tilts his head at me. "But, well, you heard that."

"I do know they, and you, are working hard, and I hope you know how much I appreciate it." With a nod I add, "And I agree with you about, you know, a happy home."

He turns to leave the small room, and I follow him to the hallway, saying, "I had to run out to the store earlier. I hope Tim wasn't a nuisance this morning when you were working in the attic."

"That was Hector up there. I've been off-site most of the morning." Victor stops at the door to a room the guys are working in. "So, is he a relative?" When I smile he hurries to say, "I mean, the way he answered the door this morning, he seemed awfully comfortable with the house, and he could take after your husband's side of the family—a nephew perhaps? Not that Mr. Mantelle mentioned him."

"No, he's not related to Craig. Or to me." Why does it make me nervous, the thought of him talking about Mr. Raines with Craig? I hurry on. "But you may have met him before. He's Amanda Raines's son. The author."

He does a double-take, then stares as he mumbles, "Amanda's son?"

"Yes. Timothy Raines. Her son."

Breaking his stare, Victor looks down. "No. We never met." He tugs on the door molding like he's seeing if it's secure. Then one of the men calls to him, and with a nod at me, he goes back to work.

Now that was awkward. Maybe Annie's theory that Victor and Amanda were more than just Shrimp Festival coworkers is right. One thing is obvious: his thoughts on having a happy home aren't just words. Now that I've met his confused, maybe even troubled, wife, his words have even more of an impact on me. Poor guy.

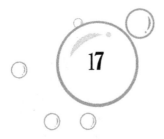

17

"So, tell me more about the Shrimp Festival," I say when Annie sits down beside me on the couch at Adam and Leesa's house. All three kids are cuddled up on top of beanbags in front of the television. Their hair is still wet from the pool, which makes me give a sympathy shiver. The air conditioning is cold even for me, and I'm not wet.

"Let me catch my breath," Annie exhales and lays her head back. Then she sits forward and stares out the sliding glass door. "And watch it not even rain now, after I ran around like a crazy woman getting those kids out of the pool!"

"The thunder *was* pretty loud." I'd come in through the side gate as she'd told me to do, only to find her arguing with the kids to get out of the pool. She sounded almost as mad as Victor Morrison was with his workmen earlier today. The comparison makes me smile.

Snuggled under blankets with their damp hair and red cheeks, the kids look like angels, but out at the pool the middle one was pushing every button her grandmother has. "That Katie might be a tad too much like you."

"Ya think?" Annie rolls her eyes, then grins. "But you think it drives me crazy, you ought to see how it ties her mother up in knots." She slaps my thigh. "But hey, thanks for coming over. I'm ready for some adult conversation. We'll get the taco bar going when this show is over. What's with the interest in the Shrimp Festival?"

"It's just such a big part of things here, and I was wondering about it. How it got started." I lean to my right and reach for the lamp. "Okay if I turn this on?" It's getting darker outside, but it's still not raining. The family room is not big, but the kids are close to the television, and Annie and I are next to each other on the couch so we can talk. I tuck one leg under the other and turn to better face my friend, whom I can now see in the afternoon gloom.

"It started with shrimp boat races back

when I was a kid, I guess," Annie says. "I'm not sure of the actual date or anything. Lucy would know all that kind of stuff. But it grew and grew even as there were fewer shrimp boats around. There's still a lot of shrimping around here, and I know I eat a lot of local shrimp, but uh, what else you want to know?" She jumps. "Oh, all the food vendors have to represent a charity. A local charity. Like one church youth group does shrimp quesadillas that are just to die for. But then pretty much all the food is." She scoots up on the couch. "Speaking of food…"

We get up with just a glance from the girls, but A.J. leaves the television and follows us into the kitchen area. He walks right into his grandma's side and buries his face in her blue, cotton pant leg. "Grandma, I'm hungry," he whines as he mushes his face around, leaving a shine of snot and saliva.

"Baby, get off me so I can get you some food. You want tacos?"

He shakes his head, still rubbing his face on her leg. "I want chicken."

"Good!" Annie says brightly as she picks him up and sits him on one of the stools at the counter. "You sit there and watch us get your supper ready."

He slumps on the counter, still whining

but also watching the television in the next room, albeit from a slanted view, as his head is resting on the shiny, tiled surface.

Annie opens the fridge. "There. You can set all those little bowls on the table while I heat this up."

Sneaking a peek at the bowl in her hand, which looks like ground beef, I wrinkle my nose and say, "Chicken?"

She smirks and shakes her head. "No, but he doesn't know or care. For some reason his parents think he should get to have an opinion as to what's on the table."

I laugh and carry an armload of matching bowls with lids to the table. "Want to use these Styrofoam plates?"

"Absolutely. I bring them from home so I don't have to wash dishes all weekend. If Meghan mentions sustainability, show her the dish soap and washrag. That usually ends that conversation."

There's a loud boom, and the lights flicker. The girls whoop and scurry to the kitchen. Annie greets them with open arms and a wide smile. "Great timing! The taco bar is now open!" There's a second of decision on whether to be scared about the thunder and lightning or excited about supper. Katie, the middle child, makes the decision by grabbing a plate and scrambling up onto a stool next to her brother.

"These baby taco shells are adorable," I say. "I've never seen them."

"Leesa orders them online. The kids love 'em." Annie stands behind her grandkids, helping A.J. hold his shell steady while he fills it with cheese. "How about some lettuce, Sugar Bug?"

A.J. nods enthusiastically while Katie, the seven-year-old mini-Annie, announces that she doesn't eat lettuce. "It gets stuck in my teeth."

Meghan tsks, as older sisters are wont to do. "Lettuce is a vegetable and is good for you. I don't eat meat on my tacos. Meat is *dead* animals."

That gets a bit of a gasp from me but apparently doesn't even register with her siblings. Her grandmother gives her a glare. "Meghan Marie—what have we said about that at the table?"

Apparently enough that the ten-year-old just lifts her chin and keeps her mouth closed. She piles cheese, lettuce, tomato, and slices of avocado onto her three mini shells. Then she settles onto the stool at the counter nearest her. I'm still in the kitchen area, facing the taco bar and the diners. Once they are eating, Annie waves a hand at me. "Help yourself. We can either eat standing here at the bar or sit at the kitchen table."

The kitchen is small but open to the living room. There are only three stools at the counter, but at the window to the side of the kitchen is a table. The window side has a bench, and there are four chairs, one each at the head and foot and two on the side facing the window.

"I'm good standing here." I wink at Katie, whose mouth is full but not stopping her from making another taco. "It's closer to the food." Katie grins, giving me an unappetizing glance at deconstructed taco.

A.J. has eaten his two tacos, and now his eyes won't stay open. His little head keeps bobbing, but Annie is nestled up behind him so he won't fall off the stool. "This one didn't get a real nap today and is ready for bed. Can you finish dinner with the girls while I take care of him?"

"Sure."

The television went through its restart protocol after the momentary electrical glitch. Now it jumps to life, and the girls shift on their stools to watch it as they eat. I top my mini taco with an avocado slice and enjoy it while looking out the window at the

downpour. This is the first real rain we've had
in weeks. Everyone's complained about how
dry things are, but it's an oddly damp dry,
not the crisp, parched dryness back home.
Everything still looks lush, but it feels heavy
and dirty. Like being thirsty while swimming
in the salty ocean.

The girls finish and migrate back over to
the beanbags. Meghan changed the channel,
assuring me they were allowed to watch the
show she selected. Such a firstborn! Never a
thought of straying outside the boundaries,
and making sure others know it. I clean up
the countertop where they were eating and
stick the bowl of meat in the microwave to
reheat for Annie and me.

When I hear her coming down the hall, I
press start, and the bowl turns in the light of
the big, old-fashioned microwave.

"Thanks for heating that back up," she
says. "Listen to that rain! Let's make our
plates and eat at the table. The girls are good.
I've worn them out today, and they've done
the same for me." We settle at the table, she
at the end so she can see Meghan and Katie,
me beside her facing the window. There's not
much to see except for a wooden fence, but
above that the sky is lighter, and the sound
of the rain is no longer as urgent. "Looks like

we're into the summer pattern of afternoon rain," Annie says. "That'll cool down some of these ungodly temps." Pushing her plate away, she focuses on me. "Speaking of ungodly, you met Fiona Greyson? I'm sure she was dragging Charlie around by the nose the way she does. The way he *lets* her do it is what kills me! That marriage is one for the books, I tell you. Aiden says none of the guys at the station can understand it either."

"But what about him saying it was a murder?" I interrupt the gossip session I feel coming on. I really don't want to talk about Charlie Greyson and his marriage.

Annie's tongue darts out and runs along her bottom lip as she detours her thoughts. "I know! Amanda Raines murdered? Honestly, I could see someone accidentally killing her, but what in the world there could be to murder her intentionally over is beyond me."

"But what about the Shrimp Festival money? And what you said about her and Victor Morrison?"

Her eyes go blank. "Money?"

"You know, Leesa and the festival books?"

Scowling, she shakes her head at me. "There's not enough money in the festival to kill for. And as for Amanda and Victor Morrison?" She frowns. "I was just playing a fool.

Can't see it. You had to know Amanda. She was so scared of everything."

"But Timothy said she *told* him she stole a hundred thousand dollars. She *told* him."

"What! How did you hear that?" Her blue eyes are as big as I've ever seen them, and her exclamation gets the girls' attention.

"What is it, Grandma?" Katie asks. The girls float over to us. "The rain stopped. Can we go outside and ride our bikes? It's not dark yet."

Grandma doesn't even look out the window. "Sure. Wear your helmets." As soon as the door to the garage closes, she leans toward me and grasps my arm. "Where did you hear that?"

"Didn't we tell you? He, uh, Timothy told me and Tamela. Tamela's husband too. Huh. You know, Martha was there and was crying and—you're right, we didn't tell you." I stand to take our plates to the garbage can. "I told Lucy, but she said it wasn't possible."

"Well, duh! Of course she's going to say that. She's one of the festival bigwigs. So what did he say she did with all the money?"

I shrug. "He thinks there's a man involved, but I think maybe he's just read too many of his books. He said sex and money are always the problem."

"He said that about his own mother? Ew."
She jumps up. "Let's go outside and watch
the girls. We'll have to keep moving so the
mosquitoes can't find us."

At the door she turns to skewer me with
one eyebrow raised. "And while we're talking
about things you've neglected to tell me...
Just when did Mr. Author-Man move into
your house?"

Oh. That.

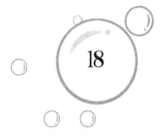

18

"They've arrested Mrs. Morrison!" Eden says after knocking on my door, hearing me mumble something from the depths of sleep, and stepping inside my bedroom.

I struggle to sit up. "What? What time is it?"

"Almost six. Aiden's on early shift and had a message when he got up."

"And he called you? This early?"

She doesn't answer, just shifts around, half shrugging, half turning away from me, though in the semidarkness I can't really see her. I sigh and roll my eyes. "Oh. He was here." We've still never really discussed Aiden staying over, and it's not a conversation I plan on having, as I've already figured out that some things are just not talked about around here. "Whatever. So, you're headed to work?"

"Yes. It's really cloudy, so that's why it's still dark. Sorry to wake you, but I thought you'd want to know." Beside the door to the hall, she stops again. "He's awake downstairs."

"Aiden?" My phone is plugged in on the other side of the bed, and I get up to walk around to it.

"No. You know." She leans toward me and whispers, "Mr. Raines."

"Oh. Him." I pause for a moment. "It's weird with him here, isn't it?"

"Yes!" she pushes through gritted teeth. Then she strides across the room to me. "He came in last night after you'd gone to bed and sat up with me and Aiden. He asked a lot of questions about you and, well, Mr. Mantelle. It was creepy."

"Aiden thought it was creepy?"

She shrugs and slowly turns back to the door. "Not as much as I did. But, you know, he's a guy."

"Okay. I'll see how much longer he needs to stay. Maybe he's about ready to leave."

Eden sticks her head back in the door before she closes it. "Don't bet on it!" She raises her eyebrows at me, then pulls the door shut.

There are no messages on my phone, but I'm too awake to try going back to sleep. Besides, I came up pretty early last night to read in bed. I dig my latest mystery novel out of the covers, where it spent the night after the last time it tumbled from my hands.

Crocodile on the Sandbank is the first in the Amelia Peabody series by Elizabeth Peters. It's set in Victorian times, starting in England but ending up in Egypt. It is fascinating, but I was really tired last night. The large paperback book's cover is colorful, though not in this dim light. I lay it to the side and stretch. Beyond the palm tree, the sky is gray, but it's not raining yet.

I google the time for today's sunrise and see if I can get to the beach in time for it. I throw on shorts and a T-shirt, hold a pair of flip-flops so they won't clack on the stairs, and slowly open the bedroom door. I creep down into the kitchen for a bottle of water. No sign of you-know-who. Water bottle in hand, I pause, thinking which way out of the house will make me less likely to run into him. I really don't have enough time for thinking, so I decide on the front door, and I'm off the porch and in my car before I know it.

Pulling through the gate, I smile in relief.

I did it! But it doesn't take even a block of travel to realize I'm being ridiculous with all my sneaking around. I must've been half asleep.

Sophia Beach is quiet. A few delivery trucks lumber along Centre Street as I come to it and turn right to head to Main Beach. Early-morning joggers and dog walkers are the only other traffic. Everything is visible now, but the sky is still a solid, early-dawn gray as I approach the bend in A1A where the famous road begins its journey down the east coast of Florida. I'd heard of A1A all my adult life in Jimmy Buffett songs but never thought about living in an A1A town. Leaving the much-sung-about road, I pull into the Main Beach parking lot and find a spot near the sandy sidewalk. There are people gathered on most of the benches facing the ocean. A yoga class is going through its poses, facing the bright smudge on the horizon. I kick off my flip-flops under the edge of one of the benches, and then, with my phone in one pocket and keys in one on the other side, I head straight for the water.

Silver water rushes to me, then pulls back. The waves are calm close to shore, but they still shut out any other noise. Wet sand sucks my feet into it if I stand still, so I begin walking along in the bubbles and the tiny, tumbling shells at the edge of the surf. Shafts of gold light are spiking out of the clouds, and then there's that first sliver of intense orange. The sun is up.

It always amazes me how fast it comes fully up. You can't look away at this moment because it goes from sliver to half to full circle in the blink of an eye. Does the earth really turn that fast? It makes a day, a lifetime, seem so short. So measurable.

Up until now my life has felt very measurable. So measurable I didn't have to think about it. School. Job. Marriage. Kids. And then…

Sparkles shoot across the water at me. The water changes from silver to dark blue, then to blue-green. The sparkles move and shorten as disinterested clouds pass in front of the sun, which, instead of being that intense, deep orange, has become the yellow sun of kids' drawings. Happy and bright.

With the sun up and that show over, I focus on walking, looking at the few shells in my path, nodding at people heading in the other direction, and enjoying the sunshine on my shoulders. Quickly, though, the sun goes from warm to hot whenever the clouds uncover it, and I turn to head back.

I resist looking at my phone until I'm in the car. It's been dinging and vibrating in my pocket, but there's nothing that can't wait. After all, it's barely seven o'clock. In the car, with the sand brushed off my feet and the air conditioning on, I take a look.

Annie is calling a meeting for this afternoon. She'll be off grandma duty at three and will be waiting on her porch for the rest of us with a pitcher of Bloody Marys. We are to "provide sustenance and be ready to figure out if Martha Morrison deserves to be behind bars. And if she doesn't then who should be???"

Now there's an invitation I bet you won't find on a card in a Hallmark store.

Last night, as we walked back and forth in the dusk in front of Adam and Leesa's house, Annie told me she wasn't happy about what she'd missed out on last week. The girls rode to the end of the street where we could see them, but we had to stay close to the house since A.J. was in bed. The thick humidity did not help her mood either. She fumed at each of us knowing bits and parts of the story and not even trying to put it all together. I'm not surprised she's demanding a meeting.

Some of the dings that my phone had been making on the beach are from Lucy saying she's not sure she can make it, but Annie doesn't appear to be accepting excuses. Tamela says she's bringing something "yummy" to fulfill her sustenance requirement. Cherry says she can't wait to tell us about the "disaster of a wedding" they'd been at in Atlanta since last week and that she's bringing fresh Georgia peaches to share.

I add my two cents, saying that I'll be there and have no idea what I'll bring yet. I lay down my phone to pick up my sweating water bottle and try to keep from splashing myself with the condensation. I've barely taken a sip when Annie texts back, to everyone of course: "Just bring stories of that hunk that's living with you!"

"Great," I grumble, and I turn off my phone. I only carried it to take some sunrise pictures, and I completely forgot. For once I almost had something interesting enough to put on Facebook.

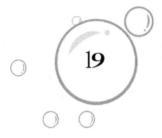

19

I pull out of the beach parking lot and head home with my silent phone and grumbling stomach. The streets are a little busier, but not by much, not even near the churches downtown, as it's too early for their congregations to be gathering. I pull into my driveway and see Timothy's car is in the same place. Eden seemed weird about him this morning, but I was sneaking around like a kid after curfew, so I can't talk. Timothy can be a lot, especially when you're counting on alone time with your guy like I'm sure Eden was last night. I chuckle, thinking of her and Aiden having to play host when they just wanted to watch their movie and make out.

Stepping out of the car, my attention gravitates to two trucks pulling into the yard.

Victor Morrison is driving the first one, and one of his guys is behind the wheel of the second. Victor bounds out and meets me in the driveway.

"Morning! You're up and out early," he booms. There's nothing in his demeanor that says his wife was arrested last night.

"Yes. I went for a walk on the beach."

"Beautiful! Beautiful!" He turns to spur his guys into action. "We wanted to get to work before it gets too hot or the rain starts again."

"Sunday? I didn't think..."

"You want air, don't you?" He shrugs. "No skin off my nose, but when I say it's a rush job, I mean it. Unless you have a problem with me and the guys being here today. Your husband said seven days a week worked for him, and you're the one we're all trying to help." He crosses his thick arms and stares at me.

"No, uh, no. I'm just surprised. I mean..." When I see he's not going to say anything about his wife, I turn. "All good with me." At the steps I look back and smile. "On second thought, it's better than good. Thanks!"

I jog up the flight of steps and am greeted by Timothy standing in the doorway.

"There you are! How do you like your

eggs?" He's beaming, hands on his hips, bare-foot and with wet hair. That pose makes him look even taller.

"Eggs? What?"

"I'm making us breakfast. Scrambled with cheese all right with you?"

My stomach growls. Loudly. "That does sounds good."

He whips around and heads for the kitchen, calling over his shoulder, "How was the sunrise? I heard you out here prowling around, but I didn't want to slow you down. You don't strike me as a morning person. More of a 'give me coffee and a walk and then I'll talk' kind of gal."

The kitchen smells amazing. Butter browning. Chopped green onions sizzling in the butter. Bread baking? "Are you baking something?"

"Reheating some bread from my mother's freezer. I ran over there this morning. It's just around the corner." He's whipping the bowl of eggs with my whisk, and he motions to the table. "Fix yourself a cup of coffee and sit down. This'll be ready in a minute."

The round table next to the kitchen win-dows has been cleaned off. It tends to catch everything I carry into the house, but now it's set with pretty placemats, cloth napkins, and pink, flowered dishes. Old-fashioned, pink stemmed glasses catch the sunshine, and then I notice the bouquet of small palm branches and pink flowers on the table. Speechless, I find the coffee pod I want and start my cup of coffee brewing.

"Can I help you with anything?" I ask as I watch him cooking the eggs, taking out the bread and wrapping it in a large drying cloth, and pulling things out of the refrigerator.

"Can you open a bottle of champagne?"

"Actually, I recently learned how to do that." I set my coffee on the table, then take the large, green bottle he hands me. The lunch bunch ladies have a fondness for champagne, so in order to be helpful, I learned about maneuvering the cork up slowly and not letting it fly off and break something when it pops.

This one pops just as he's bringing the pan of eggs to the table. They are speckled with bits of green onion, and the cheese stretches as he serves us both large portions. "Sit, sit!" he implores me.

The half loaf of bread is wrapped in a pink plaid napkin and sitting atop my wooden cutting board, which is virtually the only thing on the table that belongs to me. "Did you bring all this, all the dishes and glassware, from your mother's house?"

"That I did. The flowers are from her yard too. Why not make it more comfortable here?" He laughs, and I remember my thought to Eden this morning that Mr. Raines may be ready to leave. I also remember her feeling that I was wrong. Chalk one up for the young redhead.

"You'll love my mom's bread. It's very healthy but still delicious. Sunflower seeds, oatmeal, gluten-free…" He's slicing the bread as his voice thickens; then his words choke off with emotion. He lifts a slice to his plate and pushes the cutting board toward me.

I sneak a glance at him as I take a warm piece of brown bread studded with seeds and red berries. Cranberries, I believe. "This smells delicious," I say but then give him a minute. His head is tucked down, and he's swallowing. I focus on buttering my piece of warm bread.

After another minute or two he sniffles and asks, "How about sharing that champagne?"

"Sure." We fix our mimosas, and he lifts his glass in a toast, huskily saying, "To my mother."

"To your mother."

At that moment, Victor Morrison walks past the window and catches our attention.

"They're working today?" Timothy asks.

With a shrug, I lift a forkful of eggs. "I was surprised, too, it being Sunday." The eggs are creamy and hot. I've never figured out how some people can make scrambled eggs taste so good.

There's no longer any huskiness in his voice when he spits out, "Well, *I'm* surprised because his wife was arrested for killing my mother last night."

Now I'm the one choking. I grab my mimosa and take a sip to clear my throat, then another sip because, well, champagne can't hurt at this point. "I, uh, I wasn't sure you knew."

"Oh yes, Officer Greyson called this morning." He takes a deep breath as he holds a piece of bread up. "That's what actually made me go to Mother's." He takes a bite, then enjoys it with his eyes closed. "They found all the supplements in Mrs. Morrison's garbage. She admitted to making muffins for my mother. They often shared recipes apparently." He takes another bite and talks through it. "But tell me why my mother would eat someone else's muffins when she had a freezer full of this?"

"It is delicious." I have to admit all this talk of supplements being hidden in baked goods has taken the edge off my hunger. I focus on eating my eggs, but I can feel him stewing at my side.

Timothy chugs the rest of his mimosa and grabs the champagne bottle to pour another one. "I knew something wasn't right. I knew it, but this all, well, it feels off." He looks up at me. "Don't you agree?"

After a pause, I look at him and sigh. "I didn't know any of them, so I just don't know. But why do they think she did it? What's her reason?"

He pushes his plate of uneaten eggs away and folds his arms on the table, glass in hand. A glass into which no orange juice has been added. "Jealousy. Also something about her wanting to move back to Philadelphia where her grandkids live."

"But what would your mother have to do with any of that?"

"Who knows?" He's concentrating on the sunshine coming in through the windows and then through his pink glass. He shakes his head as he thinks, then wonders aloud, "And what about the festival money?"

"Oh yeah. What did they say about that?"

"Nothing. Didn't even mention it. That money has to be somewhere."

"Could you be mistaken about what she told you? People I've talked to say there's no money missing. That it's impossible."

He stares at me, and I can see him putting things together and trying them on for size, then discarding that idea and moving on to the next, much like I'd imagine he does when writing a story. With a deep sigh, he leans back in his chair. "Maybe I didn't hear her correctly. I mean, it's possible." He pulls his plate back in front of him and digs into the lukewarm eggs, asking with his mouth full, "Can you cut me another piece of bread?"

I do that and place it on the side of his plate. "Maybe I'll have another little piece too." I nibble on my toast and wonder how I can ask him if he still thinks his mother was having an affair. "So, the police said it was 'jealousy'?" I begin.

He chews and nods. "I think it's that damn festival. Drove all of them out of their minds. Look at this guy." He points out the window, where Victor and two of his men are measuring tubing. "His wife was arrested last night for murder, and he's here acting like nothing happened?" He reaches for the champagne. "Mimosa?"

"No, I'm good."

He pours another one, this time adding a touch of orange juice. He takes a sip, and we watch the men outside the window for a while.

"Like, just what is his story?" He stands up, glass in hand. "Maybe he and I should have a little talk." He's across the room before I can stand, but I hurry after him as he plows down the back hall and out the door. "Morrison!" he shouts, running down the steps and then again as he's striding along the back of the house. "Morriso—"

Victor steps around the corner just as Timothy gets to it. "What?"

"Your wife was arrested for murdering my mother last night."

Victor takes a deep breath and a step back. "That's right."

Timothy flings his arms out, sloshing mimosa onto the walkway. "And you're here this morning?"

"Where else would you want me to be?" Victor is an imposing man in size and manner, but not right now. His dropped shoulders, sad eyes, and shallow breathing are disarming, disconcerting.

Timothy lowers his arms, but his voice is still hard. "With your wife?"

"She had a breakdown after her arrest, and she's at the hospital. The place where she can't have visitors. You know, the psych ward."

"Oh," comes out in a breath from Timothy. As he takes a step back, I take a couple of steps forward.

"I'm sorry to hear that, Victor. Is there anything we can do to help?"

He puts his hands on his hips and looks down at the ground. Lifting his head he shakes it. "No. Just let me work."

"Of course." I reach out to touch his elbow, but he's turned away and is out of reach by the time my hand gets there. He walks around the corner, and we can hear him talking to his men.

Looking back at Timothy, I give him a sad smile. "Rough day for a lot of people."

"I hate that I did that." He dumps out what's left in his glass. "I definitely don't need any more to drink." He starts up the steps, and I follow him. At the top he steps back to open the door for me on the small porch.

"It's okay," I say. "I'm not from here, so I don't expect you to do that."

He shrugs and goes in the door, holding it open behind him. "It kinda becomes a habit when I'm here for long."

"Yeah. Where do you call home?"

"Home? I don't like to settle anywhere really." He stops in the kitchen doorway and surveys the mess he's made. "Cleanup time isn't nearly as much fun as cooking time."

I push past him. "It is for me. I'm a much better cleaner than cook. I'll take care of this. You go rest. You've had an exhausting morning."

He leans against the doorjamb and rubs his face with both hands. "Maybe I will go lie down." He looks at me through bleary, saggy eyes. "If you're sure?"

"I'm sure. Thank you again for such a treat. Everything was delicious." I head to the table and wave a hand at it. "And beautiful. It was a very nice tribute to your mother."

When I turn back to look over my shoulder at him, I'm wrapped in a full-body hug. I catch my breath, hug him back quickly, then extricate myself and move to face away from him. "Have a good nap," I say, but I don't look up at him. With my head turned away from the door, I finally hear him moving and mumbling something before he shuffles down the hall.

At the table I slide back down into my chair. My coffee is cold, but I take a sip. I also pop the last bite of bread from my plate into my mouth. Church bells ringing make me check the time. It's only eight o'clock?

The worst part about seeing the sunrise? It makes for a very, very long day.

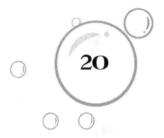

20

"You're excused, Cherry, since you had a legitimate reason to be out of the loop with the wedding. The rest of you…" Annie makes her judgment, complete with cocked eyebrow, from her oversized wicker throne, obviously a holdover from the 1970s. Which pretty much describes her entire screened porch.

Lucy lounges on the loveseat made of twigs, made comfortable with seat and back cushions of faded cotton in burnt orange, gold, and avocado green. She sighs and takes the celery stalk out of her Bloody Mary. "I'd argue with you, but Mother already dressed me down about our failure as a detective group resulting in Martha being locked up."

Tamela shoves her feet against the porch

floor to stop the hanging swing she and Cherry are enjoying. "What? Miss Birdie thinks it's our fault?" Tamela's worried frown is now topped by guilty eyes.

Lucy, chewing her bite of celery, points the rest of the stalk at Tamela. "You got it." She sits up to take a drink. "Annie, sweetie, you missed your calling not being a bartender. This is delicious. What's on the rim?"

"Creole spice. I use Tony Chachere's mixed with a bit of brown sugar. Rub a dill pickle on the rim first to help it stick." Her frown deepens. "Miss Birdie can't be more disappointed in us than I am. I've been too preoccupied, and it shocked me how much had happened that I didn't know about. So, now… where do we start?"

I raise my hand. "What made the police arrest Martha last night?" I have a big bowl of peaches in my hand, and I lean over to the table to add another dollop of cottage cheese. Cottage cheese has never been a favorite of mine, but I'm finding it's pretty good with peaches.

Annie sniffs. "Aiden stopped over at Adam's for lunch with the kids earlier. I'd bugged him all morning via text, so he folded pretty easy. Of course, the biscuits and gravy mighta helped." She grins. "Making biscuits from scratch meant we had to miss church, but I'm sure the Lord understands with Martha in jail and all. Anyway, Aiden says the police were being pressured by a couple of people. He didn't say who, but I'm thinking one of them is Eden's momma." She looks at me. "Eden say anything about that to you, Jewel?"

"Kerry Church pressuring the police? That's news to me."

"I think that's partly why Aiden talked to me, since he had encouraged Kerry to talk to the police in the first place. He doesn't want her to feel alone." Annie stretches out a hand to Cherry. "Hand me a napkin. I have to have another piece of this sausage thing. It's so good, Jewel."

"Thanks. It's really easy. Just layers of canned croissants, cream cheese, and sausage." I'd remembered the easy recipe from all the sleepovers the kids had had over the years and bought the ingredients yesterday at the store.

I thought I was keeping my face innocent enough, but Annie coyly says, "I suppose having a man sleeping over means needing to have breakfast food in the house."

My face heats up as all heads swivel toward me. Tamela slaps her thighs. "Hert is so jealous!"

"What?" Lucy asks, sitting fully upright. "What are y'all talking about? What man?" She looks at Tamela. "Hert is *jealous*?"

"Timothy Raines is renting a room from me to write in," I explain. "It's distracting at his mother's house. And tell Hert to stop by any time to see his hero."

Lucy lies back against the cushions. "Timothy Raines is a mighty fine distraction all by himself. But listen, Davis is picking me up in thirty minutes, and I have to report to Mother tonight. Y'all can talk about Jewel's love life later."

Annie speaks over my denial. "Oh, we will. We most certainly will." She winks at me. "Okay, back to Martha's arrest. Aiden helped convince Kerry Church she had information the police needed. He heard it at some dinner party Kerry and Ted threw." She cuts a look my way. "Jewel was there," she says as she takes a bite of her sausage square.

I roll my eyes. "It wasn't a dinner party. Just five of us. But she did talk a lot about Amanda feeling under the weather recently and how they'd tried to determine what was going on. She and Amanda were big buddies on the whole healthy eating thing."

Lucy leans up and pulls her crochet shawl off her shoulders. "I got the feeling the other day that Martha wasn't a fan of Kerry Church. Remember?"

Annie whoops. "That's right! She said something about her having tattoos and pulled a face, you know, like Kerry is beneath her."

Interjecting, I hold up a hand. "But that might have more to do with the business than the actual tattoos. Kerry doesn't care for Victor because he wouldn't let the tattoo parlor open a tent at the Shrimp Festival. It was interesting hearing Eden's mom talk about how badly Amanda had been feeling, but I guess I'm surprised that was enough to get the police to arrest Martha." I pause because I feel a little strange saying this, but then again, Victor did say it to not only me and Tim, but in front of his whole work crew. "Speaking of Martha, Victor said this morning she had a breakdown at the station? She's in the, well, the psych ward."

Lucy shivers even though it's very warm on the shadowed porch. She pulls her shawl back up, then holds it tightly closed in front of her. "That's why Mother is so upset. She heard from a friend at church this morning that Martha completely lost it. Saying she didn't do it. That she loved Amanda. Mother nailed me, saying Martha came to us for help and we have a responsibility to her."

We are quiet, and I believe we all feel the chill along with Lucy even though it's over eighty-five degrees in the shade. Tamela says, "I never thought of people depending on us. We're not real detectives."

Cherry gets up from beside Tamela on the swing and walks to the edge of the porch. "Sorry, but I have to move around after sitting in the car all morning." She walks a couple of yards away, then comes back. "If we help, then it's good to be depended on. That's how it is being a nurse. If you think of all that depends on you, you'll never make it through a shift. You just do your best and stay alert. I didn't meet this lady, but if she's guilty, then what have we hurt? If she's not, then…" She shrugs at us.

I nod. "There just doesn't seem to be a real reason why she'd do it. I asked Timothy this morning"—I purposely avoid looking at Annie's dancing eyebrows—"and he said he thinks the festival drove them all crazy. There has to be more to it than that, right?"

Lucy huffs. "Well, of course. I mean, it hasn't driven *me* crazy. I'm not sure I like this young man, good-looking or not."

"Welllll…" Annie drawls out. "There is one more thing." She has all our attention. "Martha believed Amanda was having an affair with her husband."

"Oh!" Tamela frowns. "So we might've been right? Victor and Amanda?"

"Wait," Cherry says, arms crossed, leaning on one of the porch beams. "This Martha is saying she 'loves' the dead woman and at the same time is saying she believes she was sleeping with her husband?"

"Not exactly." Annie scrunches up her face as she tries to explain. "Martha is telling the police she doesn't think they were having an affair, but when she was first brought in she said she did think that. She's been a little all over the place. Kind of like when we saw her at Lucy's."

"Oh wow." Tamela shakes her head. "No wonder the police don't know what to think."

Lucy stands, smoothing down her dark-gray church dress. It's short-sleeved with a simple, round neck that barely shows her collarbone. She has on plain, gray pumps and a string of pearls laying in her paisley scarf of grays and yellows. "Maybe we'll know more soon. Now if you'll excuse me, Davis is picking me up to go visit the woman of the hour."

She steps through our little circle, and at the edge she turns. "Martha asked to see me."

Annie stiffens, planting her hands on her knees. "Now why didn't you tell us that earlier?"

Lucy steps away as if she's not going to answer, then stops and faces us. "Because I know too much. I know Amanda wasn't sleeping with Victor Morrison. Because, well, because I know who she *was* sleeping with."

She turns and strides across the porch while we all watch her, waiting for one more line. One more name. But we're still waiting when she pulls the glass door shut behind her.

Annie looks around at the three of us, mouth gaping and eyes wide. "Well now if that don't beat all!" She tips her head at me, one eyebrow adding extra oomph. "Maybe there's something to that Mr. Raines's opinion on that gosh-darn Shrimp Festival after all!"

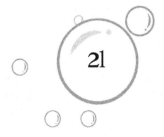

21

"I think it's the heat," I complain to Erin via speakerphone from the air-conditioned comfort of my car. "I just don't have any energy. Especially by the time I get to the end of the day." I'm parked beside an expanse of water that's swirling as the tide comes in. Annie's house is on the marsh back in the woods. The marsh has lots of moss-hung trees, sandy roads, and spots like this, where you can see the back side of the island and the sunset, although there are too many low clouds for that today.

Erin laughs. "At least I know why I don't have any energy. How did you do this, Mom? I can't imagine carrying *two* babies at one time, but even more I can't imagine having

175

three preschoolers running around while you
were pregnant with Drew."

"I did it, and I still can't imagine how! I
guess it was just a day-by-day kind of thing.
You're not too tired, right?" I pause because
I hate to nag her, but I am her mother. "No
more problems? Blood pressure okay?"

"Yes. Paul didn't even go golfing today. I
tried to tell him he should get it in before the
baby comes, but he said he wanted to stay
home and pamper me."

"Tell him he gets high marks from your
mother!"

She laughs again, but then her voice falls
and sounds a bit too casual. "Have you talked to Dad lately?"

"Yeah. Yesterday." I shift in my seat, lifting the phone off its holder and closer to me.
I frown at the phone as I ask, "Why?"

"No reason exactly. He seems to like it
there."

"You mean 'there' where he is. Not 'there'
like here with me, right?"

"I guess." She doesn't say anything, but I
can tell something is on her mind, so I wait
until she finally asks, "Do you think Dad is
having some kind of midlife crisis?"

"Maybe." Taking a deep breath, I put a
smile in my voice. "Maybe he is. Or maybe

he just doesn't want the kind of small-town life you get here on Sophia Island. He's always been on the road. He's always been so busy with his job. Like you said just now, when you four were little, his job made it possible for me to stay home with you and not have to worry about anything else. Which was enough, I promise!" We laugh, and I can hear her breathing deepen. Good. "Honey, your dad and I always said we were a good team, and we were. In some ways we still are, but, well, maybe a team isn't always what's needed."

She sniffles a bit, then mumbles, "Okay."

"You just take care of yourself and the baby. Paul wants to take care of you, and you need to let him." I swallow and admit, "I'm not sure I let your father help as much as I should have."

She pauses, and I hope she's thinking about what I said. "Okay. Thanks, Mom. Well, I better go. Paul has dinner ready."

"Okay. Love you, and give Paul my love."

"I will. Love you too."

I place my phone back in its holder and say a prayer for my girl and then for all the kids. It's darker when I open my eyes.

The water is no longer swirling. It's still and reflecting the purple sky. I turn off the car and roll down the window. On the warm air come so many smells and sounds. I'm reminded of the John Denver song "You Fill Up My Senses." That's what this island does. The never-ceasing waves on the beach capped by seabirds, foam, life. Tides filling and then emptying the land, exposing oyster beds; deep, fragrant mud; acres of grass. Animals, warm- and cold-blooded, ever scurrying, scavenging, exploring, whether it's the sand, the forest, or even the landscaped perfection. And the bugs—don't get me started on the bugs. There is just so much of everything. This place fills me up.

To the top and then some.

But now that I've thought of the bugs, I see they've discovered my open window. Turning the car back on and rolling the window up, I dial my youngest son and turn on the speaker. He answers as I pull onto the dark road. I'm not worried about driving and talking because this is never a long conversation and the road is deserted.

"Hi, Mom. Whatcha doing?"

"I've been to a friend's house all afternoon. What about you?"

"Heading out to wing night with some of the guys from the team. No dinner in the dorms on Sunday night."

"That's right. Well, just thought I'd give you a call and check in."

"Good timing. I'm walking to Matt's car. Sweet boat Dad sent pictures of. Did you go sailing too?"

That explains Erin's comment. "Nope. He's still down south. Erin said it looked like he was having fun."

"Yeah, it did. Guess it's folks he works with. How fun would sailing that thing be? It'd be so cool if Dad could rent one while we're there, but using his friend's would be good too."

"Absolutely," I say into the growing pause. I can practically hear him working out that I wasn't on that text thread and that maybe he wasn't supposed to be telling me about his dad's pictures. And plans.

"Uh, I gotta go. There's Matt. Talk to you later, Mom."

"Sure. Talk to you later."

I feel a little bad for leading Drew on like that, but surviving four kids means knowing how to get information. Erin likes to talk, so she usually gets the ball rolling. She wears her feelings on her sleeve, so she drops hints and can't help reacting. Sadie and Chris are always on guard. They never give up information until they are ready. I'll hear from each of them eventually about the pictures, but they'll set the tone and control the flow of opinion and information. Drew pays the least attention to what's going on around him, so he's usually the weakest link—if I get to him before the others have shut him down.

Yes. I was one of those parents.

The house is lit up, and I can see that both Eden and Timothy's cars are here. The windows are open to let the twilit breeze in, and there's music playing. I can see them in the kitchen, and they are laughing. I can't wait to get inside and join the party.

I never really liked boats anyway.

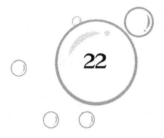

22

"So let me get this straight," Timothy says, leaning on the coffee table from his seat on the couch. He's got a piece of paper he just retrieved from the office copier, and he's drawing circles and squares on it. "This is Mom. This is Mrs. Morrison. Women are the circles. This square is Mr. Morrison or, as we're calling him, Mr. AC." He falls to the side laughing, and his head falls into Eden's lap. She pushes him upright, but she's almost too weak to do it from her own laughter.

I can't help because I can't catch my breath.

We might've done some tequila shots.

When I got here they were eating taco meat with nacho chips right from the pot on the stove. Apparently they bonded over a couple of margaritas and decided to make tacos. Then margaritas seemed too involved, and they decided to do shots. They were a mess when I got here, so I decided if Craig could go out sailing with his friends, I could have some fun too.

I did corral the food into actual plates and bowls, and full stomachs helped the situation. However, when I tried to catch them up on the murder investigation, it all went south again.

"Okay. Okay." Timothy sits up, blinks a couple of times, and bends back over his paper. "This square is the 'other man,' whom we will hear more about from Miss High-and-Mighty Lucy Fellows."

"Hey now. She's my friend."

He points his pen at me. "She's a festival person." Taking on a deep, judging voice he says, "She's not to be trusted!"

Eden grabs his hand. "Wait, where's the health food store? We need the scene of the crime!" She yelps and pulls the pen away, then slides over close to him to draw on the paper. "And a triangle for my mom. Kerry must get on the chart since she's the one who went to the police."

With the pen going back and forth between them, they work on their masterpiece.

A masterpiece focused on the murder of Timothy's mother. Something's not right here.

I stand. With a big smile, I shake my head when they look up. "I'm going to get the kitchen cleaned up and go to bed."

They groan behind me, but I just keep shaking my head and ignoring them. In the kitchen I turn on the tap and lean on the counter as I wait for the water to get hot.

Occasionally as I clean, over the music, I can hear them giggling, but the tequila is in here with me, so they aren't drinking any more. I've already put it in the sink under the cabinet, behind the cleaning products.

It doesn't take long to have the kitchen wiped down and the dishwasher running. I turn off the music and listen. Nothing.

"Oh!" Eden and I both say when we meet at the doorway, scaring each other.

"Oh no! You cleaned it all up already. I was going to help. I promise I was."

I hug the sweet girl and turn her around. "Go get in bed. You have to work in the morning, don't you?" I push her ahead of me into the living room. There's no sign of Timothy. "Has he already gone to bed?"

Eden shrugs but keeps walking to the stairs. I see her look down the hallway to Timothy's room, where a light shines under the door. When she turns back, I'm right there beside her.

"Aiden picking you up for work?"

"Aiden?" she says, a deep crease between her eyebrows.

"Where's your phone?" I ask, and she looks around. She really has drunk a lot if she doesn't know where her phone is. "Stay here," I say, and I go dig in the couch cushions where she'd been sitting. "Here it is. It's off. Is it dead?" I hand it to her, and she shakes her head.

"No. Tim thought it would be a good idea to have some downtime. No one to bother us."

I take the phone back out of her hand, mumbling to myself about Tim and his good ideas. I turn it on and wait for it to leap to life. I hold it up to her. "There. Aiden's texted you and called." Shoving the phone back into her hands, I point her up the stairs. "Go call him."

She's already talking to him by the time she gets to the top of the staircase. She wiggles her fingers at me as she disappears into her bedroom and closes the door. I glance down the hallway in time to see the light go out in Timothy's room.

I wander around, turning off lights and

making sure the doors are locked. At the coffee table I pick up the paper I'd left the two
of them working on. Sure enough, there are
all the players. Every last one of them. Well,
except one.

I don't see Timothy Raines anywhere on
the page.

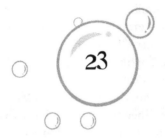

23

"He's a what?" I blurt, but the other ladies just groan and roll their eyes. "Seriously, did you say he's a 'pirate'?"

We're all crowded into Lucy's office at the tourist center and chamber of commerce. She'd told us to come over at nine this morning to hear what Martha had to say when Lucy visited her yesterday.

"Yes. He's one of the pirates, you know, that do the landing during the Shrimp Festival and set off the cannon. Surely you didn't miss that?" Lucy demands, like she's personally vested in the festival. Oh wait. She is.

I answer back with a bit of edge myself. "No, of course not. I mean, they do it, like, every two hours the whole weekend, so it would be impossible to miss. But, well, I guess I thought they were just hired actors."

All the ladies are smiling at me, but they are not all smiling at me in the same way.

Tamela is grinning with enthusiasm. She speaks up first. "I like the pirates. I think they make Sophia Island special. And they are very historical."

Cherry's smile is cynical; she adds an eye roll. "Sure. They're historical, but so is the plague. Doesn't mean we need to celebrate it. I mean, I don't really care, but they do seem a bit over the top."

Annie is squeezed next to her, and she bumps the tall nurse with her shoulder. "You don't really care now because your husband changed his mind about wanting to join them! You sure cared when he wanted to buy you a corset and a hat with a feather!" Annie cackles and leans against her scowling friend. "Alan and I loved being a part of the pirates, but I just couldn't do it once he passed. Too many memories, and I was too busy with the kids."

"You can join them? Like a club?" I ask into the hubbub

"They are a club," Lucy says loudly, "but we are off track. I do actually have work to do, you know." Everyone hushes, and Lucy nods at us. "As I was saying, Martha insists she never gave those supplements to Amanda, even though she did worry about Victor and Amanda working so closely together. That is, until I told her about Amanda and her pirate. She's completely embarrassed by what all she said to the police. It's hard to understand because she seemed pretty clear when we talked, but to hear the police, she's been all over the place."

"How does she think Amanda got those supplements if they didn't come from her?"

Lucy sighs and looks down at her desk; she looks up at me, then at Annie. "She thinks maybe Kerry Church, Eden's mom."

Annie's mouth drops open into a bright, coral-orange ring. "No! Why in the world would she think that?"

Lucy shrugs. "Martha says Kerry always thinks she knows what's best for people. That she had given questionable advice to other people. Even on health matters."

I shake my head at Lucy. "But Kerry is the one that went to the police."

Cherry bends forward to put her elbows on her knees. She's perched on a thick window ledge. "What if she gave the supplements to her but didn't mean to hurt her? What if she thought she was helping?"

Annie wrinkles her nose. "I think Martha's just snatching at straws to put the blame on someone else. It doesn't matter if her husband was fooling around with Amanda or not. Only matters if that's what she thought was going on."

A sharp knock on the door gets our attention. It opens, and the receptionist from the desk out in the hall sticks her head in. "You said you wanted me to let you know when you had ten minutes."

"Okay, thanks." Lucy nods at the young woman, who looks around the jam-packed room with wide eyes, then closes the door.

Annie fans herself. "It's getting hot in here, and you've got your meeting to get to. So, what should we do now?"

Lucy stands up. "Here's my list." She hands the sheet of light-purple paper to me and begins collecting things from her desk. "Y'all can hang out in here, but I've got to get over to city hall. Y'all take care of everything on the list. I know what I need to do." She moves past Tamela and pulls open the door.

"But wait, you didn't tell us about the pirate," I say. "Shouldn't we talk to him?"

Lucy closes the door she'd just opened and whispers, "His name is on the paper there in your hand. I guess the police didn't know about him until I told them yesterday. I hated to betray Amanda like that, but Martha was just pitiful, and I promised Mother we'd help her. I've got to go." She slips out the door and pulls it shut.

"Who is it, Jewel?" Annie asks, stretching to see the paper.

I scan the sheet, looking for a name in all of Lucy's instructions. "Here it is. Frank McNaughton." Everyone shakes their head at me as no one recognizes the name.

Then Tamela exclaims, "Oh! Isn't that Mac? You know, the guy with the food truck. Well, he used to have a food truck." She pulls out her phone. "Hert knows him."

We all wait and listen as she talks to her husband. "Hi, hon. Is the guy Mac with the food truck's real name Frank?"

Hert goes on and on, as he tends to do, but we can't make out what he's saying. She hangs up finally. "Yep. That's him. He's not doing the food truck anymore, though. Hert says he ran into Mac last week at the marina doing some pressure washing."

Annie settles back in her seat and waves a hand. "No way that's who Amanda was seeing. First of all, Mac is more my kids' age. Lucy's wrong about this."

"Here's what she says." I lift the paper and read out loud. "Yes, *that* Mac." I look up. "I guess I should've read that before you had to call Hert. Sorry. Anyway, it looks like Amanda was in charge of the pirate invasion last year at the festival and met him. She was in love. I don't know about him. Someone needs to talk to him, and someone needs to talk to police after they interview him."

Annie scoffs. "Someone is awfully bossy to not even be here. What else does she want us to do?"

I answer. "Talk to Kerry Church and also go to the health food store and look around. That's it."

Cherry stands up. "I need to go to the store anyway, so I'll do that. I assume you're talking to Charlie Greyson, Jewel? We all know he likes telling you things more than the rest of us."

Tamela chuckles. "Good idea. I'll see if Hert wants to help me track down this Mac guy. He will be thrilled to be involved."

Annie crosses her arms. "I feel kind of weird talking to Eden's mother. Unless you want to go with me, Jewel?"

"Sure. But then you have to talk to Officer Greyson with me. Plus…" I drag out the last word and pause.

Tamela has already opened the door, but as my pause drags out she turns to look back. "Plus what?"

"Something's just not right with Amanda's son, Timothy Raines."

"Like what?" Cherry asks.

"I'm not sure, but, like, where does he even live? I just think we need to look into him."

Cherry speaks up. "I'll search him out on the internet. See what I can find out."

"Good. I don't feel right doing it myself with him living in my house, you know?"

Cherry pats my back. "No problem. I'll let you know what I find. Did Lucy mention when we should get together again?"

"No. But I'm busy tonight," Annie says. "Maybe just get together a little early for lunch on Wednesday?"

"Good idea," Tamela says from the hallway. "We're going to Colby's, and being early will help with getting parking spaces at the marina. I'll text Lucy so she'll know."

We clomp down the old staircase and move onto the sidewalk. It's still in the shade from the morning sun, but the day is already heating up.

Annie groans. "And I thought it was warm in there. Let's go see if Kerry's in the shop yet,

Jewel. Then we can track down Charlie and see if the police have talked to Mac."

We all split up, walking in our separate directions with our assignments. Once we are away from the others, Annie bends closer to me. "I'm not supposed to tell anyone, but I just have to tell you. Leesa says there *is* evidence that money has been taken from the festival!"

"What! When did she tell you?"

Annie steps away from me and shrugs. "*She* didn't actually tell me."

"So, how do you know?"

Sliding her eyes at me she smirks. "My kids know I don't babysit on short notice except when it's an emergency. So Adam had to tell me where they were going to get me to agree to go over there tonight. Especially when I asked if the reason they needed a babysitter was because they had an appointment with a marriage counselor."

"Annie! That's awful!"

"Well, it's not my fault he wouldn't tell me outright that Leesa has to meet with this accounting guy the police brought in."

"Sounds serious." We look both ways at the corner, then cross Centre Street on the brick crosswalk. We skirt around salespeople setting up their merchandise and signs on the sidewalk. Racks of T-shirts and boxes of sharks' teeth hold less interest for us than the gauzy outfits outside one store and the advertised shoe sale at another. Eventually we make it to Signs, the Churches' tattoo parlor. The neon OPEN sign isn't lit yet, but we can see Ted inside, and when we pull on the door it opens.

"We weren't sure you were open yet," I say.

"Oh. Thanks. Kerry is always fit to be tied when I forget to turn that on. She's got me a list of opening chores to follow, but what can I do for you ladies? Ready for that first tattoo, Miss Jewel?" He winks at me as he weaves around us to turn on the bright, red-and-blue sign. "Annie, Eden says you're still thinking about that dolphin?"

"What?" I say. "You're thinking of getting one?"

Annie sniffs at me and raises an eyebrow. "One? What makes you think I don't already have a tattoo? Or two?" She follows Ted farther into the shop. "Ted, tell me what you think about Amanda Raines getting herself killed. Do you think it could've been an accident? Someone just trying to help her get to feeling better?"

Ted stops on the other side of the cash

register and frowns at her. "Good Lord knows it wouldn't be the first time the police in this town jumped to the wrong conclusion." He lifts up his hands, palms out. "Now, don't go getting mad, Annie. You know I'm not talking about Aiden, but you and I grew up here, and you know what I'm saying is the truth."

Annie shrugs and looks away from him, at some pictures on the wall. "Can't argue with you. So, you think it could've been an accident, though? What's Kerry think?"

He lifts his hands again. "Oh, I can't say what she's thinking. You know better than that. My wife has her own mind." He looks at Annie's back as she studies the pictures, then looks to me and shrugs.

I smile and ask, "Is Kerry here? Upstairs maybe?"

His eyes dart to the staircase, then back to me, but he doesn't say anything. In the quiet, Annie turns to look at me. "I guess I've just not made up my mind on the dolphin." She makes a circle, looking around her, and then walks past me to the front door. "Jewel, let's come back later, okay?"

"But…" I'm pretty sure Kerry Church is standing in the shadows at the top of the staircase, but Annie has already opened the door and is waiting for me, so I wave, saying over my shoulder, "Okay. Ted, tell Kerry we said hi."

"Will do!" he calls as I swivel and hurry after my friend, who is already on the sidewalk.

"We were supposed to talk to Kerry. I'm sure she was there," I whisper at Annie as she lets the door close behind me.

Annie nods in my direction, but she veers off to cross the street in the middle of the block. "She was most definitely there, but I remembered something. Come on!" she demands when I hesitate. "My car is this way." There's very little traffic this early, but we still cause cars to stop for us. I wave and smile at the drivers while Annie barrels on.

She pulls her keys out and points the clicker when we approach her car. "Get in. We need to go see my lawyer."

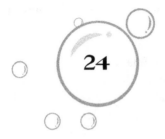

24

I sit carefully on the hot leather seat of her car. I've learned that just because it's early, it doesn't mean the car isn't already hot. I tug on my tan linen shorts to cover as much of the backs of my legs as possible, and sit forward. Annie has on slacks, so there's no need for her to be careful, and by the time I get settled, she's pulling out of the parking place.

"Isn't your lawyer your daughter Abbie?"

"Yes. She's also Ted and Kerry's lawyer."

"She can't tell you anything about them."

Annie gives me a 'duh' look and frowns. "Of course she can't!"

Pretty self-righteous for a woman who just tricked her son into spilling the beans by talking to him about his possible marriage problems.

She drives out of downtown and turns right on A1A. We drive almost to the bridge that leaves the island, but then turn left into a small office park with cute buildings and signage. We weave around the curvy streets and park in front of Bryant Family Law.

"Hey," Annie says, closing her door and stepping onto the sidewalk. "You'll get to meet Annabelle. She answers phones for Abbie when she's not in class."

"Good. She's the only one of your kids I haven't met."

However, when we open the door and step inside, we are not greeted warmly by the youngest Bryant. "Momma. What are you doing here?" the stunning young woman behind the desk asks. She has honey-blonde hair in long waves, Annie's bright, blue eyes, and broad, athletic shoulders. She rushes to get out from behind the desk to stand between us and the hallway.

I try to squelch a giggle. Looks like the youngest Bryant child has this job because there's no way a stranger could stop Annie Bryant. Annabelle doesn't leave her post but sticks out a friendly hand to me. "I bet you're Mrs. Mantelle. I'm Belle Bryant."

"Annabelle Bryant," Annie corrects her.

"So good to meet you. Yes, I'm Jewel."

The young woman shakes my hand and winks at me. Then she plants her hands on her hips but does not move or smile, only cocks her head at her mother. "Do you want me to give her a message?"

Annie retreats to one of the two high-back armchairs in the reception area. "No, thank you. We'll wait. Have a seat, Jewel."

Annabelle huffs, crosses her arms, and frowns. Then a door behind her opens. She jumps, Annie stands, and I settle in for the show. Voices fill the hallway as Abigale tells a man goodbye. He passes us, nodding at Annie, then gives Annabelle another look as he pushes open the front door.

"Mother," Abbie says. Then she looks at me and smiles. "Hello, Mrs. Mantelle. Can I help you with something?"

"No. I'm just riding along with your mom."

"That's what I was afraid of." She turns to her sister who is back behind the desk. "Belle, how much time do I have?"

"Five minutes. Ten at the most."

Annie tips her chin up, then marches down the hall, waving at me to follow. "Her name is Annabelle, and since you never have more than ten minutes to talk when I come here, I'm amazed the walls aren't papered in gold. You must be making money hand over fist."

I smile at the girls, who roll their eyes at each other.

The walls might not be papered in gold, but the office is very nice. Varying shades of gray walls and navy- and white-painted furniture make it look very modern, comfortable, and coastal. We sit in two chairs like the ones we just left, and Abbie slides behind her desk, which looks like a table. I've noticed that's the trend now, but it makes it hard to slip off your shoes and relax.

Annie laments, "Since I only have fifteen minutes, I'll hurry. Mostly I just need your memory. Kerry Church and Martha Morrison. About five years ago they had a falling-out, Martha was doing some kind of downtown do-gooder thing, and Kerry tried to hire you to stop her? You remember?"

Abbie nods, then swivels around to grab a bottle of water out of the small refrigerator behind her. "Either of you want a water?" We shake our heads, and she closes the door. "I do remember, and she never paid me for the advice." She leans back in her chair and stretches her legs. She's large like her mother and has a full head of dark hair. She wears it in a braid most of the time. She has on a

silky, white, short-sleeved blouse and a nub-
by, dark-red suit skirt. Her matching jacket is
hanging on a rack beside the door.

"Honestly, I didn't give her any advice she
should've paid for. It was mostly two bossy
women each wanting their own way. It was
something about the front window at the
old tattoo shop. Martha Morrison wanted it
uncovered so you could see what was going
on inside. Something about how ordinances
where they came from didn't allow for covered windows."

"Oh, good gravy," Annie groans. "Another one of those 'that's not how we did it up
north' folks."

Her daughter shrugs. "Pretty much.
Something about visibility helping with
crime and some other stuff, but from what
I remember she went straight for Signs because they had a tinted window in the old
place and because Kerry argued with her in
public at some meeting. I told Kerry Church
that Martha's group didn't have any legal
standing, so she should just ignore them. Of
course she mostly just ignored me instead
and wrote weekly letters to the newspaper
and shot her mouth off at every town meeting for a few months. Eventually it all just
went away."

"But they apparently are still holding on to the animosity. That could be important now, with Martha in jail charged with murder and Kerry being the one who went to the police," I say.

"Doesn't surprise me. They were both confident they'd never been wrong about anything." She stands up. "Is that all you wanted? I do have an appointment."

Her mother gives her a slanted frown. "Whatever," she says, but she doesn't get up. "How are you? How are things on the farm? With Mark?"

Abbie looks at me, then smiles and shrugs at us both. "It's marriage. It's hard, but the kids are happy."

I stand. "I'll go out front and wait for you, Annie." Ignoring their objections, I dart out into the hall. "Just giving them a minute to say bye," I say to Annabelle. Or Belle, as she prefers it.

The pretty girl sighs. "Momma misses Abbie and the kids. She and Abbie are really more alike than the rest of us. Consequently, Abbie doesn't know how to draw any boundaries with Mom, so the rest of us try to run interference."

"I noticed earlier. Do you work here much?"

"Not really. I graduate at Christmas and hope to get a full-time job then."

"Around here?"

She looks down the hall. "I guess. I mean, if my mom has anything to do with it."

"What do you want to do?"

She straightens up. "Broadcasting. Sports preferably." Then her face falls. "I know. Not likely I can stay on Sophia Island, right? Oh, here she comes." She meets her mom in the hallway and hugs her. "Y'all going to lunch?"

Annie grins. "Probably, and then home to clean, clean, clean! Love you, honey, and see you for dinner. Let's go, Jewel. I feel like Mexican food." She pushes me out the door and into the heat.

I open the car door. "I thought we were going to track down Officer Greyson."

"Of course we are, but if I told Annabelle that, she'd already be on the phone with Aiden." She gets in and starts the car. "Sometimes, Jewel, my kids are a royal pain."

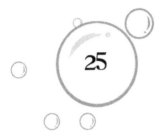

25

"No, we're not seriously looking at Mac," Charlie Greyson says as we walk alongside him at the marina.

He was headed to Colby's for another officer's retirement lunch, but he said he'd give us a few minutes if we got there quickly. We stop along the graying railing. He leans against it, his back to the water, and we stand in front of him. The sun is warm, but there's a good breeze coming off the river.

"This wasn't a one-time act of passion," he continues. "It was a systematic poisoning over several weeks. So, what is it you have to tell me about Kerry Church?"

Annie twists her mouth, then says, "I hardly feel like you've told us enough to warrant an exchange of information. Is it true about Mac and Amanda? That they were, you know…"

Charlie looks around. He's wearing his white uniform shirt; with it pressed and tucked in, he looks more official than usual. He smells good, and his tan really stands out against his shirt. When his gaze shifts to me, I realize I'm staring. I quickly look out at the water.

He clears his throat, then nods at Annie. "I believe so, but you never heard anything about them?"

"No. Not a word. I wasn't real close to Amanda, though, and she wasn't from here, so people didn't talk about her as much." She shifts her weight and leans a hip against the railing. "About Kerry, she had it out for Martha. They've been feuding since way back, remember?"

"So, you think she'd lie about her?"

Annie's nod is enthusiastic. "I do. Jewel does too."

"What?" I blurt. "I have no idea. Why would you say that?"

My friend's mouth flies open. "You said not five minutes ago that you didn't trust her. That something didn't feel right."

"But I didn't say I thought she lied to the police."

"Same difference," Annie says, but Charlie asks over her, "What's off about Kerry Church to you?"

"I don't know. She just seems sneaky, and well, I don't know."

Charlie folds his arms and studies me while I try to think, which is hard to do with him staring at me.

Annie leans toward him and whispers, "She also feels that way about Timothy Raines."

"Oh, you do? And yet you still let him move in with you?" His eyes narrow at me.

"Not with me, exactly." I chuckle, then swallow. "I mean, you know that. He's writing a book."

"So, what feels off about Mr. Raines?"

Taking a deep breath I try to come up with something other than saying I don't know again. But… "I don't know. Just something."

My fidgeting stops when Charlie leans toward me. "Trust your gut. There *is* something off about that guy." He raises an eyebrow. "When's he moving out?"

Annie chimes in. "Why? Ya jealous, Charlie?"

He backs away from me like I'd just stuffed a firecracker into his shirt. "No!" he practically shouts. "Anyway, I have to go." He turns away from us without even a goodbye.

With two long strides, I catch up to him and grab his arm. "Did she give the festival money to that Mac guy?"

That stops him. He looks from me to Annie, then back again. "Nobody is supposed to know about the money. We're trying to keep it quiet." His eyes narrow again. "But now that you two know..." He shakes off my hand and heads to the restaurant.

I stare after him and spit, "How dare he insinuate that we can't keep a secret!" Flinging around I catch Annie with a wrinkled nose and a guilty look.

She lifts her shoulders and grins. "He might've meant me more than you."

~~~~~~

"She never told me she was that old."

Mac keeps coming back to Amanda's age, which isn't endearing him to the three women trying to talk to him. Hert is trying to steer him away from the age thing but not having much success.

"Buddy," Hert tries again. "Forget that. She was a good-looking woman." His eyes flit up to his wife with a quick apology. "So, how long were you and Amanda together?"

"Ya mean each time?" Mac squints up at Hert from his crouching position on the floating dock.

Annie and I had talked to Officer Greyson on the other side of the marina, on the north side of Colby's. Most of the boats are anchored along the floating docks on the south side of the restaurant, lashed to the pilings in the middle of Sophia Beach Marina. After Greyson left for lunch, Annie got a text from Tamela saying Hert had discovered Mac was there pressure-washing the sides of the docks, so we met them here to talk to him.

It's not going well.

Hert stammers, "No, uh, no, not like that. How long, you know, in weeks or months were you together?"

Mac laughs. "I know, man. It was just too good to let pass." He stands up. "Let's walk over here in the shade. It's about time I took a smoke break anyway."

We follow him to a picnic table in the shade of the marina building, and we all sit down. He pulls out his cigarettes and offers one to the rest of us.

Hert answers for us. "No, thanks. So, the police talked to you this morning."

Mac is a stocky, well-muscled man with thick, dark hair and a full beard. He's wearing work boots, jeans, and an old T-shirt. His wrinkled face above the beard looks to be more from the sun and from laughing than age. He's told us twice that he's barely forty.

"Yeah. I talked to the police. They said Amanda was sixty-eight. That's almost seventy." He takes a long drag. "She sure didn't look that old."

Annie takes a deep breath. "Mac. Forget her age. It's not like she was ancient!" When he opens his mouth she shuts it with a glare. "Were you still seeing Amanda when she died?"

There's a bit of a grin playing around his mouth, and I suddenly realize he's not as stupid as he's acting. "Sure, Miss Bryant, I'd see her around town, but you probably mean the way old folks talk around sex, saying things like 'seeing' and 'been with,' right? Sure, I was *seeing* Amanda right through the festival. She liked my pirate garb." The grin unfolds. He leans his head back, and we all see Mac the Pirate come to life.

"Oh my!" Tamela lets slip.

He stands up as he pulls on his cigarette. Then he flicks it off into the gravel and blows out a stream of smoke. "Amanda treated me good. She loved to cook me these great big meals, and a guy's gotta eat. And, I hafta say, I

213 KAY DEW SHOSTAK

treated her good. Gave her what she wanted. But that was it. I guess she might've wanted more, and I told Officer Greyson that. She said I could move in with her, so if I'd been after her money I could've had it. She was a nice woman, but she wasn't real grounded in reality, you know?"

"No, I don't know," I say. "What do you mean?"

He looks down and laughs again. "Well, there is the pirate thing, like I told you, but she also talked about buying a sailboat. Sailing off on it." He looks around. "No idea if she'd even ever been on a sailboat—matter of fact, I'm pretty sure she hadn't by the things she said—but she went on and on about it. Gotta get back to work." He tips a finger wave at us and walks back toward the docks. Then he turns around. "And, oh yeah, she also talked about her son being some famous author. Crazy stuff like that."

Hert yells, "But he is! Timothy Raines."

Mac stops and puts his hands on his hips. "Huh?" He gives us a leer. "Whatever. But I wasn't really there for the talking, you know?" With a big laugh, a very big pirate laugh, he strides back onto the docks.

None of us really have anything to say.

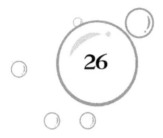

26

"Mom can't say just yet."

Eden is wadded up in a chair in our backyard the way young people do. I'm sitting in the same type of fold-up, nylon chair, but my feet are on the ground, and my arms are resting on the armrests. The drilling inside the house has chased us to the shaded yard, which heavy cloud cover and a stiff breeze have made somewhat comfortable. The breeze is also keeping the mosquitos at bay.

"I just want to know why she's so sure Martha killed Amanda," I reply. "I mean, if it's that silly grudge over the store window coverings, the police won't hold Martha much longer."

Eden stretches her arms high above her. Her legs remain twisted beneath her. "She says that old stuff has nothing to do with it." Her phone chirps, and she lifts it. "That's her now. Wants to know if she can come over." Eden starts tapping on the phone, then puts it back in the chair's cup holder.

"What'd you tell her?"

"To come on over and bring something to eat."

I stretch and then push myself out of the chair to stand. "I'll leave my chair for her then. I'm going inside. They can't be working much longer."

"No. She's coming to talk to you. Specifically."

"Me? Why?"

"Don't know." She also stands. "Let's get some drinks and bring a little table out here." She looks around at the clearing in the midst of our jungle backyard. There are old pavers barely visible beneath the dirt and grass. The lawn people finally cleared the backyard enough to mow out here last week, and this area looks like it might be where a gazebo once stood. Trees circle the edge of the pavers, leaving a nice, open, shady spot.

"Okay," I say, and we walk toward the house. "What's your mom bringing to eat? Annie and I never did get lunch this afternoon, so all I've had is an apple."

"Who knows? Mom loves cooking and feeding people, so it'll be good. They've always got a fridge full of yummy stuff."

We enter the house by the back door and can hear Timothy in his office typing. No, not his office. Craig's office. Or—whatever. We're putting together a small cooler of ice, glasses, a bottle of wine, and some water bottles when I move closer and whisper to her, "Should we ask Tim to join us?"

She scrunches her face together and shakes her head. "I'm not sure Mom will even talk with me there, much less Amanda's son." We carry our cooler and basket to the back door and down the stairs. We hear Tim on the phone, or talking to himself, as we pass the office again. Eden sets the cooler down. "I'll get the table from the front porch," she says. She talks to someone at the corner of the house for a minute; then Victor comes around the same corner alone.

"So you ladies are going to have a picnic. How nice!" He's sweated through his light blue sport shirt, and his thick, dark hair is damp. "I won't stand too close because I must stink to high heaven. Just wanted to let you know we're done for the day. We might have you some cool air by tomorrow. Next day at the latest."

"That's great to hear! How, uh, how are you doing?"

"Oh, good. Hard work is good for the mind and the body." He smiles big, his signature look, but his eyes are sad. He sniffles and looks down. "It's all good. Just glad you guys are going to have cool air soon." Lifting his head he flashes that bright smile again. "I'd better go. You have a nice night."

I think of offering for him to stay, but I have no idea how much food Kerry is bringing. Plus, Eden said she only wanted to talk to me. As I turn toward the spot in the yard where our chairs are, I hear Kerry and turn around to see her hugging Victor. She backs off, though she's still holding one of his arms. Eden comes up, lugging the small table, and joins their conversation.

I decide it's none of my business and continue on my way. Kerry and Eden soon join me.

"I just wish he'd stayed," Kerry says with a sigh, setting her canvas bags down. "Hello, Jewel."

Eden deposits the table in the middle of us, then runs back around the house, saying something about a chair and the cooler as she does.

It's a little awkward, since I think Kerry

was eavesdropping on Annie and me as we talked to Ted earlier today, but then she grabs my arm and steps close.

"Before Eden gets back, I need to apologize for this morning. I'm sure you knew I was there, but I just didn't feel like talking at that minute, and Annie, well, dear Annie can be a lot that early. I'm sure you understand."

"Sure."

As we begin setting things on the table, I think we can both feel that her apology did nothing to clear the air. It might even be more awkward now.

Eden lugs a third chair around the corner. Victor brings up the rear, hauling the cooler with two strong arms. "Here we go," Eden says. "Mom said I could stay for your chat, so I needed a chair." She turns to Kerry. "What did you bring?"

"My bread with a couple of cheeses. Crab spread and sliced cucumbers too." Her mass of hair is knotted up in a low, loose bun with wisps around her face. She's wearing a sleeveless dress of faded yellow cotton and a pair of white tennis shoes.

"I'm just dropping this off," Victor explains. "You ladies enjoy yourselves."

"Thanks, Victor. We will," Kerry says. She stands to give him another hug.

She has to stand on her tiptoes to hug him, and that's when I remember her saying she barely knew him when we had dinner at her and Ted's apartment. I remember because she mentioned he hadn't lived here long, though I knew he'd lived here at least ten years. She also didn't seem to like him very much.

I wait until he's around the corner before I blurt out, "I thought you didn't know Victor Morrison well and that what you did know, you didn't like."

She doesn't look up, just keeps setting the table. "That was before, and I still don't know him well. But now I know, well, enough."

Eden's head is cocked at her mother. "What does that mean?"

"That I know him well enough to know he's having a rough time. His wife is in jail for murder after all. Let's sit. This is just lovely out here. I believe I'll even have a glass of wine, sweetie." She looks up at me and my surprised face. "Yes, I know we turned away your gift of wine, but it's for Ted's sake. He's not allowed to drink, so I don't."

"Mom! You make it sound so bad. He doesn't drink because you don't let him."

Kerry reaches for the bottle of wine and pours it into three glasses. "Exactly, but

Eden, I don't want to talk about all that. What should we toast?"

Eden is fuming, and her mother is acting oblivious, so I say, "To having air conditioning!" We all toast, then dig in like we haven't eaten in days.

"Jewel," Kerry says as soon as the wine and food are no longer the center of our attention, "I don't want you to think badly of me. You are a dear friend of my daughter's, and I hope we can be friends too. I want you to know why I believe with my whole heart that Martha Morrison killed my friend Amanda."

Eden's eyes are wide, and she leans forward on her little stool from the front porch. She's only a foot off the ground, so it's like having a child at our knees.

I nod. "Okay. That would be helpful, I think."

Kerry holds one hand over her heart and looks down. The gray day has only grown grayer, but the rumbles of thunder are in the distance. A few frogs have begun to chirp in the surrounding trees, and the breeze is picking up. Finally she takes a deep breath and looks at me.

"Amanda. Dear, lonely Amanda was having an affair." She motions with her quickly emptied glass at her daughter, who is seated closest to the bottle of wine.

"Yes. I heard that," I mumble.

Kerry gasps and, ignoring her daughter's pouring, turns to me. A splash of wine hits the ground instead of her glass. "How could you have possibly heard that? I've told no one!"

Her response causes my mouth to clamp shut, and I shrug.

She studies me, then fervently shakes her head. "No. I don't know what kind of gossip you think you might have heard, but it isn't true. No one but me knows about Amanda and Victor!"

"Amanda and Victor!" Eden and I say at the same time. As far as I know, Eden doesn't know about Mac and Amanda. I mean, I didn't tell her, but Aiden could have, I guess.

Eden shakes her head. "Seriously, Mom. She was, like, really old, and he's married!"

Okay—if that shocks her, she definitely doesn't know about Mac.

"Young lady, just because someone is older than you, it doesn't mean they're dead. Amanda was a very vital woman. A lonely woman. And every marriage is not fulfilling and loving like your dad's and mine. And

Martha Morrison is a bitter, controlling woman who's made Victor's life a living hell!"

Her cheeks are flaming, and her red hair seems to fairly crackle. Her shoulders jut out of her sleeveless dress, and she snaps her eyes back and forth between her daughter and me, daring us to disagree. Then she seems to remember my earlier statement, and an air of curiosity overtakes her anger.

"So, tell me what meaningless gossip you heard about Amanda. As I said, I'm the only one that knew about her and Victor. He was completely ashamed, so I know he told no one else."

"Uh, no. Maybe it was about someone else."

She sniffs. "If it's about that pirate, that was just lust."

Now Eden really gasps. "Pirate?"

Kerry sniffs again, more directly at me this time. "Yes. I can see you know about that." She rearranges her skirt, looking down to where it lays against her freckled legs. "I'm surprised the whole world doesn't know about that." With a shrug, she sighs. "She was lonely."

"But I thought you said she was seeing Victor?" As I say that I remember Mac laughing at how we old people soften the thought of someone having sex with our innocuous words, and I can't help but smile.

"Why is that funny?" Kerry demands. "If you only knew what Victor has gone through. Amanda just couldn't dump him when she fell for that boy toy. You just don't know what he's been through."

Eden's eyes are popping out of her head, but I manage to keep my smile to myself this time as I solemnly ask, "What exactly has Victor gone through?"

"Exactly? Well, he only shared that with Amanda, of course. Let's just say men aren't allowed to fight back."

Her daughter leaps off her stool. "Mom! Are you saying Mrs. Morrison was abusing him? Are you kidding me?" She looks back toward the corner of the house, where she'd talked to Victor only moments ago.

"Sit down. Don't be so dramatic." Kerry rolls her eyes at me, then looks back at Eden. "You young people think you have the world figured out when you've not seen a fraction of what really goes on." She motions for Eden to sit down again. "Open that container in the bag there. I brought us each a piece of my baklava."

Eden does as she's told, the promise of

baklava easing her umbrage at her mother's opinion.

My brain feels like it's caught in an ocean of crashing waves, the kind where you can't come up for air without another one breaking right on top of you. I need to get away and think all of this through. But not before dessert, of course. "Thank you. This looks heavenly."

Kerry smiles. "I like mine with just a touch more cinnamon than usual. It's one of my favorite things to make and share with my friends. Amanda was one of my biggest fans." She takes a bite and chews. Her look of delight turns to a frown, and since I think the baklava is fabulous, I don't know what the frown is about.

She sees my concern and, as she swallows, shakes her head at me. "Ignore me. I'm just thinking about Amanda. That was the only time we fought. I found out she'd given the box of homemade baklava I'd given to her to that Mac! The whole box!"

She is busy taking another bite when Eden screeches, "Mac! Mac is Miss Amanda's pirate?"

Looks like Eden and I are caught in the same riptide.

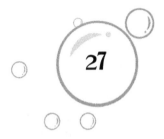

27

The clouds finally released their burdens around five. While the afternoon in the backyard had begun pleasantly, as the humidity built, so did the awkwardness of Eden's questions about Amanda and Mac and of Kerry's over-the-top support for Victor. After we finished our baklava, packed up Kerry's bags, and put the chairs and tables away, even a newbie to Florida could feel the rain on its way. Eden left to go to a girlfriend's house, Kerry giving her a lift before she hurried home. I grabbed my phone and a bottle of water and plopped down in a chair beside one of the front room's windows.

The window is in a corner of the room far from the kitchen, tucked away so that the fireplace and television can't be seen from it.

I'd never appreciated how many unusable places there are in old houses. Maybe they made sense at one time—a home examining room for a doctor or maybe a storage place for firewood or a warm place for a baby to sleep during the day. Then another generation comes along and takes down the walls and doors to make more living space, creating odd, out-of-the-way nooks.

This corner would be good for reading, except there are no electrical outlets, so there are also no lamps. The two windows are big, though, so there's usually good daylight unless a thunderstorm is moving in. Eden placed two of the more comfortable highback chairs here, so it's a good place to sit beside an open window and look at my phone.

The side yard is fairly open, not like the jungle out back. It looks out over the intersection our house sits in the corner of. There are big trees ready to bloom along the edge of the black iron fence. They have naked limbs reaching up to heads of leaves and clusters of small pods, much like a lilac bush, except these trees grow huge. I like how they provide a kind of a barrier to the street, but I can still see through them. The grass is thick on this side of the house. Now that it's getting mowed regularly it looks even thicker. There are squat palm bushes around the perimeter that I think are called palmettos. From this view the yard looks almost like it's cared for.

The wind picks up, pushing in the window and causing me to lean closer. The tops of the trees are swaying nosily, and then I realize it's not just the wind I'm hearing. Rain is coming.

I've never heard rain coming in any other place we've lived. It's like a stampede of wild animals are headed this way, and then I can't see much beyond the window. With such deep eaves, I'm only getting a little spray from the rain, but the smell makes it worth it. I love the smell of rain, and these afternoon storms are deeper, warmer, more overwhelming than any other rain I've ever enjoyed. Leaning my chin in my hand, I close my eyes and relax.

"Did I snore?" Timothy asks.

I startle awake to find him struggling to also wake in the other chair across from me.

We laugh as we stretch and yawn. It's obvious we were both sound asleep. I say with a yawn, "I don't know if you snored. I didn't even know you were in here. I guess we were both tired from last night."

The drizzle provides a backdrop of sound along with the runoff from the eaves, and we finish waking up as we look out the windows. He settles deeper into his chair. "You were really out of it when I came in here. I was done for the day, so I shut off my computer to enjoy the storm. I came here looking for you, though it took a while to find you."

"Now that we've gotten the windows uncovered and cleaned, it seems like this house has more nooks than I realized." My words pause naturally, but then I push myself. "Can I ask you a question?"

"Of course."

"How long have you been in town?" He opens his mouth to speak, but I jam my second question in. "You were here a few weeks ago, weren't you?" His mouth shuts, and he cocks his head. I push on again. "You've been here the whole time. You were here before the Shrimp Festival."

Now he leans forward, elbows on his knees. He pulls his hands up to cover the lower part of his face, and he turns to look out the window while I wait.

"I was in and out." He looks at me. "Why?"

"Where do you live?" Cherry had done her assignment and sent me Timothy Raines's information earlier. His place of residence is Sophia Island on all his social media.

He shrugs, then rubs his face with his hands before sitting back. "Mother had been letting me stay with her. I was in between houses."

"For how long?" I raised four teenagers; I can tell when someone doesn't want to tell me the whole story.

"A while. My latest books aren't doing well. This one is going to get me back on track. It's historical fiction, which I've never done, but it's going really well. You want to read some of it?"

"Really? That would be…" I slow myself. Yeah, he's distracting me to change the subject. I recognize the tactic well. (See above re: raising four teenagers.) "That would be great. So, you were living with your mother."

"Oh no." He stands up and walks around the small area. "No, she wouldn't allow that. She had other plans." He stops, with hands on his hips, to stare out the open window.

"Plans to move Mac in?"

"How did you know about that?" He had jumped a bit like he was going to turn around, but his smooth voice tells me he decided to play it cooler.

"I heard it from a couple of sources."

We're both quiet, with him staring outside and me trying to think through this whole thing.

He turns around and drops into the chair. His chin juts out, and his eyes are harder. "Mother was selfish. She had all this money and wouldn't even help out her own son."

"The money from the Shrimp Festival? But I thought you said she didn't have it. That she stole it for someone else."

He scoffs. "Come on. If she stole it you don't think she couldn't have gotten her hands on some of it if she wanted to? Or gotten more?"

My eyes widen, and I can see he knows he went too far.

"I don't mean that she should've gotten more for me. I just mean she didn't, uh… she could be selfish at times."

"Why didn't you want people to know you were living here? Hert said you weren't around, but the bookstore guy saw you on the beach."

After a long sigh and a pause, he sits back. "I might as well tell you. Mother has a guest cottage behind her house. I'd been staying there without her knowing. In the middle of the festival and the preparations leading up to it, she was rarely at the house anyway.

She'd kicked me out so she could have her pirate around, but I figured she didn't use the guesthouse, so I might as well."

"You can have the whole house now. Why are you living here?"

"Don't you believe me that I'm writing a book set here?" He looks and sounds offended.

"I believe you. But… come on, it's a little weird. We don't even have air conditioning."

He scoots forward, even drops one knee to the floor, then reaches out to take my hands. "Jewel, this book has to be a success. Writing is all I know how to do. You said it yourself, I'm a good writer. I have to figure it out, and I just can't think over there. Over at Mother's house. It's just too… too much."

He pleads with his words, his knee on the ground, and his eyes.

Pulling my hands away from his, I straighten up. "Okay. I get it." I shift toward the window, where shafts of sunlight hit the raindrops clinging to the grass, the trees, and the Spanish moss. "Rain's over. I have things to do." Moving my legs, I spur him to get up off his bended knee. I avoid the hug he tries to give me by scooting around the other side of the chair and scooping up my phone from where it had slid down the side. "There's my

phone. I'm going to return some calls." With
a smile I hold it up. "I turned the ringer off
so I could hear the rain. And doze!" I laugh
and hit my stride on my way to the kitchen.
He's in my tow but being quiet.

At the first door into the kitchen, he
stops. "Guess I'll go get a bit more writing
done. I really am making good progress."

I give a cheery "okay" without looking at
him as I put away the glasses and dishes I'd
washed after my late lunch with Kerry and
Eden.

He moves down the hall, but then, at the
back kitchen door, he sticks his head back in.
"And Jewel? I was serious about you reading
some of the book."

Again my "okay" is cheery and said without a glance his direction. I don't stop my
busyness until I hear the office door close behind him. Then I melt into the first chair I
find.

Where my mind felt pounded by waves
earlier, now one thought is pulling me down
into a whirlpool. He sounds guilty. He looks
guilty. He's acting guilty. That's the only ex-
planation I have for him not being at his
mother's house.

He's guilty.

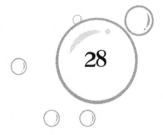

28

"I just couldn't be in the house alone with him any longer."

Annie shudders. "Well, of course not! You don't have good luck being with murderers when the jig is up." She spikes an eyebrow at me, and I swallow.

"Maybe I've developed some sixth sense or something because my skin was crawling. I couldn't get out of my house fast enough."

Annie and I are standing on the front porch of her son Adam's house, watching the kids ride their bikes. A.J. is riding an old-fashioned tricycle on the sidewalk while his sisters zip by on two-wheelers with their friends. "Five more minutes!" Annie calls, then says to me, "You coming in?"

"No. Thanks, but I'm going to talk to the police about everything Timothy said."

She winks and gives me a nudge. "The police? Or Charlie Greyson?"

"Or maybe your son Aiden? Ever think about that?"

She clouds over. "Well, shoot. I wanna be there if you're talking to Aiden. I can pick up what he's thinking like a snap."

"Next time. I'm going to ask Aiden to stay at the house. I mean, he's there most..." I swallow guiltily before continuing. "...or do you not want to know about that?"

"I definitely do want to know about that. I'm glad he's there for both you and Eden as long as Tim Raines is there, but please, pretend you never told me. I'm holding out for that boy to put a ring on it, and I'm of the good old school of 'why buy the cow if you can get the milk for free'!" We laugh, and then she hollers, "Kids! Time to go in!"

"I'm right here, Grandma," Katie says with all the weariness a seven-year-old tasked with managing the world can muster.

"Oh, good for you. Good listening, honey," Annie praises her granddaughter.

Katie shrugs and turns into the open garage. "I always listen." As she takes off her pink helmet, she squints up at us. "Are Uncle

Aiden and Eden getting engaged? And what kind of milk does he get for free? Is it like the little cartons we get at school?"

"Hi there. Thanks for meeting me."

Charlie waves his hand at the rest of the bench facing the marina, where we'd met earlier today. He's sitting at one end, watching the sun sink below the clouds.

I did talk to Aiden, but it was on the phone on my way here, so I didn't exactly lie to Annie.

As I sit, leaving a wide space between us, Charlie says, "No problem. I owe you an apology anyway. You are not a gossip. Annie, on the other hand, has been known to be less than discreet."

I chuckle. "She said as much. But that's neither here nor there. I talked to Tim Raines this afternoon. Did you know he's been living here on Sophia since before the festival?"

As his face pulls southward, I can tell he didn't know. "Where?"

"His mother's guesthouse. She didn't know either."

Orange light shoots through the parting clouds, and I watch him think. "He told us he was homeless, but he made it sound like it was somewhere else. Now that I think about it we asked pointedly about his mother's house, and he answered just as pointedly that he had not been staying in her house."

"So he could've, uh, he could've done it? Right?"

"Killed his mother? I guess. But why would he?"

I can't help it. I look around to make sure no one can overhear. "Money. I guess he's broke. His books aren't selling, and he says writing is the only thing he's good at. I assume he inherits everything." With a pause, I look away from him. "Speaking of money, and at the risk of making you mad again, why aren't you at the meeting with the accounting guy and Leesa Bryant right now?"

He grunts. "Johnson took it over. Thinks I'm too easy on folks from here. He hates that everyone knows me and I know them and their families."

"Seems to me that could be an asset?"

"Ya think?" His sarcasm is thick, but then he laughs. "Honestly, I already know what they're going to discover: a bunch of money is missing. Who cares—well, except for the committee—how much down to the exact penny? I'm good with a big, round figure like a hundred thousand."

"Lucy thought it was impossible that much could be taken."

"I'd imagine Lucy is finding out differently right about now."

"Oh. I didn't realize she's there." The sun slips behind some even lower clouds, and the orange light disperses into peach and gray.

"Yep. It was my idea to have all the committee members hear about it at one time. Keep it off the official gossip merry-go-round for a minute." With the sun hidden, he twists to face me. "So is Mr. Raines still staying at your place?"

"Yes. But so is Aiden now."

"Good." He looks at his watch. "I think this is a good time to talk to Mr. Raines." He stands up. "Maybe I'll drop by and see if he's around."

"But he'll know I talked to you!" I protest.

He looks down at me. "That's exactly the idea. You don't want him thinking you keep secrets for him. Especially from the police, right?"

"I guess not. But won't he be mad?"

Charlie winks. "Maybe he'll be mad enough to move out." He starts to walk away, saying in his wake, "Why don't you wait about an hour to go home?"

I watch him cross into the parking lot beside the marina, and then I turn to face the water. It's taken some getting used to things not cooling down with the setting sun. In Illinois I carried a jacket if I was going to be out at dusk or later. There's not a chill in me at all tonight as I relax into the warm breeze. I'm still in the white, tight-legged capris I've worn all day. Topping them, my long, salmon-colored cotton sweater was a bit warm in the sun, but it feels perfect now. In the shadows on the water, I see a dolphin come to the surface, and I stand to watch from the railing. Other people veer to the railing, too, as the word spreads. No one is in a hurry, as dolphins are sighted pretty regularly here, but still, it's a dolphin.

Amanda Raines doesn't sound like a very happy person to me. She was infatuated with Mac, and he was practically laughing at her. I don't care what anyone says; I bet she stole that money for him. Not exactly for him, but to hold on to him. But then her and Victor? I wish I'd known her. I'm having trouble picturing all this—not that I want to picture everything! Good Lord, no!

But what kind of guts do you have to have to steal that kind of money from a charity? I've got to rethink my picture of Amanda Raines. She was infatuated with a young pirate. Okay, she was sexually involved with a young pirate. Mac is right: I much prefer softer, kinder words. Maybe that's part of the problem. I take a deep breath.

Amanda Raines was a thief. She was having sex with a young man and fully engaged in some pirate fantasy. She was sleep—no, she was also sexually involved with her friend's husband. I chuckle a bit. No wonder she got herself killed. I recently read *Evil Under the Sun* by Agatha Christie, and her famous detective Hercule Poirot's opinion is that some people lead lives that tend to get them killed.

My phone vibrates in my back pocket. Pulling it out I see it's Lucy. "Hello?"

"Are you at home?" she asks.

"No. Down at the marina. Why?"

"Oh good. How about a drink at the Turtle Shell? Upstairs. I'll be there in a minute. Bye!" she says as she hangs up.

I was wondering how to kill the next hour. This is perfect. There are still pools of light on the river that reflect the light purple and silver sky, but when I turn away from the water, I see that night has fallen behind me. Downtown the lights are on, the architectural streetlamps and the tiny, white lights in the trees. Store windows shine and beckon.

People walking, talking, laughing, eating give the scene life, even more so as I begin to cross the parking lot toward the Turtle Shell. Both floors of the old, wooden building have big windows open to the night breeze. Flashes of color from the televisions high on the walls add color but no sound. Tiki torches dance and beckon to me on the path outside. At the road, I look before crossing and again as I step over the railroad tracks. In front of the bottom story of windows, bracketed by the tiki torches, I pet the head of the large, concrete turtle statue, which is wearing strings of beads as if he just returned from Mardi Gras.

I don't talk to the girls out front with the menus but head up the outside staircase. Upstairs is first come, first served, but at this time on a Monday night, we should be fine. I slowly pass an open table, scoping out the seats at the railing where there's a wide plank for plates and drinks. It faces out over the marina, and I know it's Lucy's preference. I mean, why wouldn't it be?

There are two stools together at the end, so I claim them and order a Corona with a lime. Lucy shows up the same time as my beer, and she orders the same.

"Goodness knows I should probably be asking for a bottle of the hard stuff after that meeting, but I do need to keep my wits about me!" She lifts herself up onto the stool; then, with her elbows planted on the plank and her face held in her hands, she drinks in the marina laid out in front of us. "This. This is why I do what I do for this place! Law, I love living here. There ya go!" she says as she takes her ice-cold beer from our waiter. She shoves the lime down in it and holds it up. "To Sophia Island!"

"To Sophia Island!" I repeat. We take swallows, but before I'm done she's holding hers back up for another toast. "Okay, what now?"

She draws in a deep breath and straightens her shoulders. She runs a hand through her short, streaked-blonde hair and grins. "To the newest chairman of the Shrimp Festival!"

"Who?" I ask as I pull my bottle down a bit.

"Me!" She finds my bottle and taps it with hers. "Yep. Me."

"But what about Victor?"

She shrugs as she drinks, then shakes her head again. "Poor Victor is literally a shell of his former self. Evidence against Martha keeps piling up, and she's apparently getting crazier and crazier. It's just killing him. His business is probably going to go bankrupt because he's trying to raise money for her lawyers." She stops herself and tips her head toward me. "He said for me to tell you not to worry one little bit. Your house will have air before anything happens to his company."

"Poor guy. I hate that he's having to worry about our house, but I appreciate that he is." I cross my legs and lean closer to her. "But what about the meeting? The money?"

She flashes her big eyes at me, and I see they are filled with tears. "I can't believe it. Just can't believe it. She really did steal that money from us. I thought I knew her. I mean, well…" She looks around, then whispers, "That whole pirate obsession was wacky, but I thought she was just sowing some wild oats. Mac is rather appealing to a certain kind of woman. She's not the first."

"You?" I spit out, along with a dribble of beer.

"Shut your mouth, Jewel Mantelle! Of course not!" She actually crosses herself—though I don't think she's Catholic—and takes a long swig. "No. Definitely no. But some older women just can't resist their romance novels coming to life."

"Do you think she gave the money to Mac?"

Lucy sighs and stares at the floor for a minute. "Maybe? But I don't think he'd be able to hide it if he had that much money." She looks up with a grin. "He'd be okay for a bit, and then he'd be down at the Sea Snake, drunk and bragging. He's not the kind that can be smart for any extended period of time."

She's wearing a green, palm-print button-up shirt with the collar popped to frame her face. Her straight skirt is dark green, almost black, and longer than many of the skirts I've seen her wear. This must be one of her business outfits, and sure enough, she's wearing tan pumps instead of strappy stilettos. She wears high heels virtually all the time, but some are more drastic than others.

"So, what I wanted to talk to you about…" Lucy pauses to wave at our waiter and to hold up a sign for two more. "Now that I'm the chair I'm going to need people I trust to help me out. You've just got to get involved in something, you hear me? I will not let you just drift along until you end up involved in some godawful endeavor that doesn't help anyone and that isn't any fun!"

"Oh, Lucy, you know I'm just not good with things like this. Besides, I agreed to offer up the house for the Christmas tours! Let me get more settled in."

She beams at the waiter and takes the two perspiring bottles from him. "Here we go." She hold up her bottle and clinks it against mine. "To us. Being so good together!"

I try to pull my bottle away before she clinks it because I have a feeling that in Florida a clinked beer bottle is pretty much as good as a signed contract. "Wait! No, what do you mean?" I manage to blurt out before that sound of glass against glass.

She leans over and squeezes my knee. "You're just going to be my helper. My assistant. No big thing, just give me a hand." With a wink at me, she swivels on her stool. Of course she knows the folks down the bar from us. Of course she held them off until she got her main order of business done.

Which was me. Me being her Shrimp Fest gofer.

This ended up being a really costly beer. I might as well enjoy it.

As soon as those second beers were gone, we tried to leave, but it's just not that easy when you're with Lucy Fellows. The news of her being the new Shrimp Fest chairman has already hit the streets, so there were congratulatory, and consolatory, drinks to turn down. Walking past the turtle with his beads shining in the torchlight, though, it's just the two of us. We walk to the corner where Centre Street crosses the railroad. Her car is down toward city hall, and mine is in the marina parking lot, so we stop at the corner.

"Listen, Lucy," I say. "You knew Amanda well. Did you hear of her being with anyone besides Mac?"

"Like, *being with* being with? No. Why?" she demands.

She's significantly shorter than I am, but she gets taller when she wants something. I take a couple of meandering steps toward the crossing. "No reason really. But really? Nothing?"

"Oh. Are you talking about Victor Morrison?" She crosses her arms and gives me a disappointed-teacher look. "No. Believe me, that was just made-up gossip. Martha was extremely jealous of the time Victor spent on the festival. She didn't get into all the social things like Victor did, and she couldn't resist picking fights with people. She always had a tendency to tell tall tales, never more so than since she's been arrested. Ask Charlie, and he'll tell you. Apparently she hated it here and just wanted to move back up north where their grandkids live. Like I said, ask Charlie."

I look down the dark railroad tracks, and she stares up Centre Street as our conversation fades. I want to tell her that Kerry says Victor and Amanda were an item—there's another nice way to say it—but I also don't want to break that confidence. I don't think that would change Lucy's mind one bit. I don't think she has a very high opinion of Kerry Church.

Lucy picks right back up where we left off. "Besides, Amanda drove Victor crazy, and not in a good way. She was really a nervous sort. Couldn't make a decision to save her life." She sighs. "Guess that's one reason I find it so hard to believe she stole that money. As ornery as she could be, she was also tenderhearted, a real softy for animals or people in trouble."

"Except her son. She kicked him out of the house."

"Who told you that? She talked about him constantly. When he was coming to town she'd bake and cook all week. She had to have all his favorites."

"Apparently she chose Mac over him and

told him he had to leave. He was virtually homeless."

She stares at me openmouthed, then snaps her lips shut. "Impossible!" She checks her watch. "Oh my word. It's almost ten. Mother will be waiting up for me." She grabs me in a hug. "Bye, sweetie, and thanks so much for helping me out with the festival. We are going to have so much fun!" She scurries off to her car, and I join a group crossing over to the marina parking lot, which has pretty much cleared out by now.

And here I thought I'd made so much progress today with new information from Kerry and Tim. But new information doesn't matter if it's all a bunch of lies.

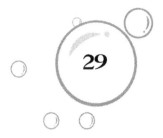

29

"Today's the day!" Victor greets me through his open window as he pulls up in the driveway. I'm on the front porch enjoying a cup of coffee as no one else in the house is awake yet. "By the end of the day there will be cool air flowing in the Mantelle mansion for the first time ever!"

He spends a minute gathering things from the front seat of his truck and then jumps down to the yard where I'm waiting for him. After a night of tossing and turning, I decided I'd go to someone who should know how to straighten out at least one of the lies I've been told.

I left my cup of coffee on the porch and took my courage, and questions, to the yard. "Then it sure is a good morning. You look like you're ready to go." My courage stutters for a minute, but I cross my arms and plant my feet. We are having this conversation. "Uh, you feel better than you did yesterday? How is your wife?"

"Yes, ma'am, I do feel better. I, well, I decided to not go see Martha last night. I'm sure you wouldn't understand, but we didn't have exactly a loving relationship." His eyes wander to the house, then back to me, and he nods as he stares, chin square and eyes focused. "Well, maybe you do understand— some. You and Mr. Mantelle have some issues, I believe."

"But... no, nothing..." My hands fly up as if to make him understand, since I'm gagging on the words I'm trying to say. "I mean, we're, uh..."

"Oh. No, ma'am, nothing like ours. I was just saying you understand how a couple can come to not see eye to eye on things." His words are not the only thing retreating. He backs away from me. "Sorry. I'll get to work."

"No. I'm sorry. I asked, and I am interested." This seemed so much easier when I was lying in bed rehearsing last night. "I'm just wondering about Amanda and why what happened to her, well, happened to her, you know?"

He sighs again. "I do. I do know, and that's another reason I didn't go see Martha last night." He looks down and clears his throat. When he looks up his eyes are full. "I think she did it. I think she killed her because of her, well, her jealousy. Completely unfounded, but powerful nonetheless."

Oh, here's my chance. My heart is beating out of my chest. "Jealous because you and Amanda were, uh, together?" Forget Mac and his judgment of old people and soft words. There's a time and a place for them.

His eyes widen, and his mouth opens and shuts a couple of times. Then he gasps. "No! Not like that. Mrs. Mantelle, I would never cheat on my wife. Never! You can't go around saying things like that!"

There's real fear on his face. He puts his head down and plows around me toward the house, leaving me beneath the swaying line of palm trees, stunned and alone.

Cherry and I are seated in a booth at A1A Diner. It's a large place on the corner of A1A and Statler Drive. It only serves breakfast and lunch, but it's very popular from the full parking lot I've often driven past. We have plates of pecan waffles and are eating like we haven't been fed in a very long time.

Cherry holds up the cup of extra pecans she asked for. "Do you want some of these? I always get extra. Aren't they good?" She's sprinkling pecans on her waffle and then adding more warmed syrup. "Martin has forbidden us from coming here while he's dieting. Poor guy loves these."

"I can see why. Is your daughter still living with you? Did she decide what she's doing about going back to school?"

She flashes her dark eyes at me. "Yes. Jo is here to stay. When we moved here five years ago, she had a fit about us leaving Atlanta. Swore she'd never even come visit us here. Now we can't get rid of her!"

I laugh. "What's she going to do here?"

"She's looking into culinary school and maybe getting a job at one of the resorts. She's putting in résumés, and I hear the resorts have job fairs." She pushes her plate back and pulls her cup of coffee toward her. "I'm so full. Now we can talk. So, there's a man you think has been abused by his wife. What do you want to know?"

I push my plate back, too, even though there's still food on it. I couldn't fully enjoy it with my mind focused on this conversation.

"Does it really happen? He's not a small man. He's not what I'd think of as a weak man either."

Cherry nods at the waitress, who comes to pick up our plates. She waits for her to leave. "That's what people think about spousal abuse, but it's not always the case. The victim is rarely the shrinking violet we imagine. Men particularly work to not appear that way, and so it gets brushed to the side. I've seen it at the hospital. When a woman's been abused, we kind of all assume we know what happened and go from there. Of course the police have to get to the bottom of things and get the details, but when it's a man? I really can't remember when I've heard a man in the emergency room say his wife or girlfriend did it. Often you just feel it. The poor guy will just look terrified that someone is going to figure it out."

"That's what happened. He looked absolutely terrified." I think back to Victor's face. I hadn't known what to do when he hurried past me. Then his crew showed up, and I called Cherry because I needed to talk to someone about it.

"So, this is someone you know?"

"A little."

"Are you wanting to get him some help?"

"Oh. Oh no. I don't think it'll be a problem anymore."

Cherry presses her lips together and nods. "Okay. That's good." Our eyes meet, and I think she knows who I'm talking about. Then she gives me a sad smile that confirms it. "Yes. I think he'll be okay." We finish our coffee but don't have a lot more to say.

While we're waiting to pay our bills, Cherry takes a small bottle of hand sanitizer out of her purse. "I've gotta get rid of this maple syrup smell before I go home. Martin's grouchy enough when he's dieting; no need to poke the bear." She offers me a squirt, and we are rubbing our hands when the hostess comes to the counter.

We assure her everything was great and then head outside, to our cars at the end of the sidewalk.

Cherry says, "I'm glad you called me. I hope I helped some."

"You did. I was so surprised, I guess, which is kind of embarrassing, but I just wanted to talk to someone."

"No need to be embarrassed," she says, putting an arm around me for a side hug. "Men being abused is not something that people talk about much. But you know, this is the second time I've had a friend ask about it in the last couple of days. I have a feeling it might be about the same person."

I stop walking and turn to her. "Really? Who else asked you?"

She presses her fob to unlock her car and looks over her sunglasses at me. "Lucy. Lucy called me yesterday afternoon."

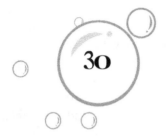

30

Lucy is in meetings all morning, so I can't talk to her. I still don't understand why Victor says Martha was jealous of Amanda, but I'm hoping Lucy can shed some light on that. At the house Victor and his crew are all busy, and I'm staying out of their way. Especially Victor's. Poor guy. As soon as I think that, I know that's a big reason abused people don't want everyone to know. Who wants people to pity them?

Timothy is gone, though not for good; his stuff is still here. Eden and Aiden are also out of the house, so after wandering around for a bit, I decide there's no reason to hang out here in the heat. I should go walk off some of those waffles. And pecans. And syrup.

Upstairs I carefully step around tubing

and wiring in the hall outside my bedroom. My tennis shoes are beside the bed, so I sit down to take off my sandals. I can hear the guys in the attic. I can't believe we'll have air conditioning tonight. It's really not been so bad having the crew here. Maybe getting the other renovations we need won't be that big of a hassle.

There's a door to the attic at the end of the hall near my room, and I hear footsteps coming down the stairs behind the door. I sit still, hoping I won't have to face Victor, then breathe a sigh of relief when I see it's the wiry, younger guy, Hector. He picks up the tubing in the hallway and gives me a wave and a nod as he heads back up the small stairway. He calls over his shoulder, "Ma'am? Can you close the door behind me? I know Mr. Morrison said you and your guest needed your privacy."

A flash of embarrassment heats up my face, but I yell back, "Sure." When I finish tying my shoes I bounce up and go to the open door at the end of the hall. I check to make sure he's clear of the door and close it. I'm sure Victor just meant they weren't to be too loud.

I hear him at the top of the stairs saying, "I'll sure be glad to see the end of these hot attics! I'm spending the rest of my days in air conditioning!"

I decide to walk on up the steps. "Thought I'd see how things are up here."

A frown flashes across Victor's face. "Are we being too loud, Mrs. Mantelle? We don't want to interfere with your company."

"Of course not. I don't have company here anyway. Mr. Raines is working, and Eden is helping me out with furniture." I push out a little laugh. Why does it bother me if they think I have company?

Hector's eyes leap to his boss, and Victor looks back at him. "Okay. Just want to keep Mr. Mantelle, and of course you too, happy."

That's it. Craig's told him about me having company. He doesn't like that I have friends. This time it's more than just a flash of embarrassment flooding my face as I turn and jog down the stairs. I can't believe Craig is talking to strangers about our marriage!

I've got to get out of here. Glad I'm ready to go for a walk.

It's a pleasant, low-humidity day, perfect for a walk. At least, that was what I thought when I left the house. The breeze has died, the sun has climbed higher, and the puffy clouds have disappeared by the time I've walked a couple of blocks through our neighborhood and turned toward Centre Street. On the first corner I come to the fudge and ice cream shop. Usually the smell alone is enough to make me consider a stop, but I'm still full from breakfast, so I walk on. I consider a stop in the bookstore, but it looks like there's a children's story hour in progress. Then I know where I want to go, so I make an abrupt turnaround and find myself hurrying, even in the heat.

"Hello again!" Ted Church calls out from behind the workstation where he's got a young lady in the chair. "I knew you'd fix on the perfect tattoo and come back." He looks down and winks at his client, then asks me, "How can I help you?"

"Is Kerry here?"

"She's still upstairs. You want to leave her a message?"

"How about I just run up and talk to her?" I ask, but I'm already at the foot of the stairs.

A shadow crosses his open face, and then he shrugs. "Sure. I think that'll be fine. I better get back to this."

I run up the stairs so that I can hardly draw a breath by the time I get to the apartment door and knock. "Kerry? It's me. Jewel."

She opens the door, and I drag myself inside. "It's too hot to be out walking," I splutter. "What was I thinking?"

"Here, let me get you a glass of water. Sit down." She has on a silk robe with a matching gown underneath. Her hair falls practically to her waist and is full of life, curls and frizzled places and kinks in a sedate red. As sedate as red hair can be. Especially this mane. She's also barefoot, I notice, as she sits on the other end of the wicker couch from me.

She spreads her arms. "Excuse all this. I just got up. I'm a late sleeper."

"Oh. Oh, that's nice." Of course I can see from her face that she thinks I don't think it's nice at all. And I guess she's right because I've never understood people who sleep late. It's got to be almost eleven o'clock. Then I smell it. Sweetness. Honey. Chocolate. Looking around I see where the smell is coming from—sheets and sheets of biscotti and baklava and cakes. They are balanced everywhere.

"You've been baking," I say, my eyes roving from tray to tray.

"All night. Can you say stressed? Actually, did you know 'stressed' spells 'desserts' backward?" She reaches over to the coffee table and lifts a piece of brownie off it. "Want a bite?"

"I'm still... well, a bite." It's deliciously rich and dark. "What is it all for?"

She looks around and twists her mouth, still chewing on her larger bite of brownie. (Not that I'm keeping track.) "I don't know. I was just worried last night."

"About Victor?"

That snaps her attention back to me. After an exaggerated swallow she nods. "I just can't get him off my mind. Two days ago I couldn't stand the man, but..."

"But you said you knew about him and Amanda. That they were, uh, having sex."

She scrunches her nose. "That sounds so harsh. I said they were having an affair. Which wasn't exactly true, but it's more true than that they were just having sex. Victor hated himself for confessing it to me."

"You know exactly what you wanted Eden and me to think. And we did think that. Why?"

"I want Martha to rot in prison for what she did to Amanda. And for what she's done all these years to poor Victor." She gets up from the couch and tiptoes to the door that leads downstairs. She pulls it open only an inch and looks down. "Good. He's got a customer."

She floats back to the couch, hair and robe flowing behind her. "Ted still despises Victor, and I could never tell him what that woman was doing. Ted simply wouldn't believe it!" I think of how Kerry bosses her husband around, and I'm not so sure Ted would find it that much of a stretch.

Then her phrasing hits me. "Wait, you said two days ago. What happened two days ago?"

"I went by your house to see Eden. She left those pants for me to hem when you came for dinner, if you'll remember, and I wanted to return them. Plus, I wanted to see all the progress she, and you, have made on the house. It was Saturday evening, and no one was there. Well, Victor was. He didn't see me at first. He was alone on the front porch, sitting in one of the chairs to the side. I didn't want to see him, but, well…" She frowns and reaches for another piece of brownie. Before she gets it to her mouth, she blurts, "I couldn't help it. He was on the phone, stammering and apologizing and, well, crying. A grown man just sitting out in the open crying. Granted he thought he was alone, but still."

She eats the brownie, shaking her head and remembering.

"Sounds awful."

"It was," she finally says. "I tried to just sneak away, but he stood up near the end of the conversation and saw me. I couldn't just leave him there like that." She clears her throat and sits up straighter. "I figured it all out that night and went to the police. Of course"—she looks sheepishly at me—"Victor says he and Amanda never had a physical relationship, that it was more of a spiritual one. But with his one protector gone, I felt I had to step in and make sure that woman never sees the light of day!" Then suddenly she crumbles and is sobbing. "The way poor Amanda wasted away—poisoned!—all because of Martha's insanity. How cruel can a person be!"

I move over to rest my hand on her back and let her cry. After a bit, through her sniffles, she explains the trays of goodies. "I couldn't talk to Ted about any of this, so I baked. And baked. And baked." She shudders and eats the rest of the brownie as I move back to my end of the couch.

With a deep intake of air, she throws her hair back. "I knew we'd be good friends. I just knew it." She jumps up. "You must take this with you. I'll pack everything in a box."

"All this? No. What would I do with it?"

"It doesn't matter. I just have to get rid of it. Take it to Victor and his workmen. They're still at your house. Give Aiden some for the police station. I told Ted it was all for a big order, so it can't stay here."

She's whirling around, packing up the baked goods and talking about each of them. It's all very surreal, and then she's got the boxes in big, cloth bags that she's hanging on me as she practically pushes me out the back door and down the outside stairs.

As I struggle down the first few steps, she leans out the door. "Jewel. Jewel, look at me."

So I do. She actually looks better, calmer than when I got here. She's holding a coconut-chocolate bar—a big bite out of it in one of her cheeks—in her right hand and a spatula in her left. "Jewel. Thank you. Just having all that out of here is letting me breathe. I pour all my emotions into my baking. No one sees me like this. No one but you now. We are truly kindred spirits." She blows me a kiss and closes the door.

And all this time I thought Eden's dad was the weird one.

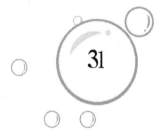

31

"Your mother did not kick you out of her house."

Timothy spins away from his keyboard in Craig's office chair and faces me. "Well, good morning to you too! Aren't you all fired up about something." He reaches for his coffee cup and stands. "Good time for a break." He gallantly bows and waves his hand for me to proceed him out the office door.

In the kitchen I lean against the sink and watch him select his coffee pod and start the machine. He goes to the refrigerator and takes out the loaf of bread he brought from his mother's. "Can I toast you a piece?"

"No. I went out to breakfast. Where were you this morning?"

He looks up sideways from slicing the

bread and cocks a smile at me. "Why? Did you think I'd been taken into custody after your talk with your policeman friend last night?"

Oh yeah. I kind of forgot about that. It's been a busy morning. "Well... *should* you be in custody?"

He puts two pieces of bread in the toaster and groans as he pushes the lever. "Jewel, what do you think? That I killed my own mother?"

The sounds of the men working on the next floor reassures me, but I slide toward the back kitchen door anyway. I don't really think he poisoned his mother, but he lied for some reason. "You lied! You lied to me about your mother." I drop my crossed arms and plant my fists on my hips. "Lucy says there's no way Amanda kicked you out. That she bragged about you all the time!"

He leans forward and sniffs the warm air rising from the toaster. "Mm, love that smell. Guess I'm going to have to learn to make Mom's bread." As it pops up, he jumps back and laughs. "Hand me a saucer, will you?"

I grab a saucer from the cabinet behind me and walk it over to him. He places the toast on it and then motions with his head for me to carry it to the table. He says, "I'll get my coffee."

At the table I sit down. He sure isn't acting guilty now like he was last night.

He slides into his chair. "As a matter of fact, I must say thank you. You sent the very person I needed to talk to my way." He looks up at me, eyebrows raised with a wide smile. "I just didn't know it." He takes a big bite of toast and seems to thoroughly enjoy it.

"No butter?" I ask.

"Nope. I want to enjoy this all on its own. I wasn't joking when I said I need to find her recipe and learn to make it."

He's so obviously enjoying the bread that I sit back and watch him. There are fewer things I enjoyed more as a mother than watching my children enjoy the food I made for them. Especially my sons. They'd come to the table starving. Before they'd even sit, they'd feast with their eyes. As they'd pile homemade macaroni and cheese or mashed potatoes or meatloaf on their plate, I could feel their anticipation. Then those first bites. Those groans of appreciation and then silence as they filled themselves. Tears from my memories run down my face. They are joined by tears for the woman who baked this bread, who will never watch her son enjoy it again. I wipe them all away and know he didn't see.

Because he's eating. And remembering.

He stares at the empty saucer. His shoulders droop, and his voice is husky. "Yes. I lied about my mother. She never kicked me out." Clearing his throat, he takes a sip of coffee and straightens up.

"I was hiding from her. You may have figured out by now my mother was difficult at times. Intense, obsessive, prone to fantasies." He holds up his hands, palms facing me. "Do not mention the pirate thing, okay?"

"Okay."

He folds his arms on the table. Raising one eyebrow at me he asks, "Do you know Officer Greyson's wife?"

"What? No. I mean, I've met her, but you can't say I—"

He cuts me off with a laugh. "It wasn't an accusation. I've heard she's difficult, and I'm thinking that's how he knew what to say."

"Oh, well. Maybe." My face feels hot, so I jump up to get a bottle of water. When I sit back down he stares at me, a smile working around his face.

"I see." He winks. "Greyson's a good man. Anyway, back to me. I told you about my money problems, which were just a part of my bigger life problems. I might've inherited some of my mother's ability to fantasize. Good for writing fiction, not so good for having a decent life—or money in the bank. So, anyway, I was hiding out in her guest cottage. Okay, avoiding her. She was preoccupied with the festival and that Mac guy, so I knew I'd get away with it. Plus…" He pauses and grits his teeth. "I'm ashamed about this part, but I was secretly looking for the money."

"Oh, from the festival. Did you find it?"

He shakes his head, then gets up to take his plate and cup to the dishwasher. "No money. That's kind of the reason I had to move over here after she died." He wets the dishcloth and squeezes it. "She was gone and I could search to my heart's content, right?" Wiping the counter harder than necessary, he adds, "Wasn't that what I wanted all that time? I didn't even notice her getting sick because I was hiding from her and obsessed with finding the money. Then she was gone, and well, I had to get out of there. Her house felt haunted."

"I can see that," I say and wait as he finishes straightening up.

He folds the dishcloth and lays it on the edge of the sink, then leans against the counter. "That's where I went this morning. To her house. To ask her forgiveness and make peace."

"I'm glad to hear that."

"So. I'll be out of your hair today."

"You're moving back there?"

"For a couple of days. Then putting it on the market and leaving town." He claps his hands together and walks into the living room.

"What?" I scramble up and enter the room from the front door of the kitchen. "But what about the book you were writing here? About this house?"

He grimaces. "Historical fiction? What a crock. I can't write that stuff. Thrillers are my game, and the online market is huge." He shoots his fingers at me like a gun and strides down the hall toward his—uh, the office. "I was just packing up when you came in."

Sure enough there's a suitcase on the bed, and the office is put away. Empty. Just like Craig left it.

"You can have Mother's dishes that I brought over for our breakfast that morning. I brought a couple of other boxes of stuff I thought you might like, so I'll leave them in the bedroom. Maybe they'll make up for me lying and wanting you to feel sorry for me.

Like I said, I'll be at her house for a day or two, but then I'm out of here. That's where Officer Greyson offered me the biggest help."

"What? He offered to help you move?"

"Nope." He zips up his computer case. "I'm no longer a suspect. He got some information last night that nailed the case shut on you-know-who's little wifey." He points upstairs where we can hear Victor and his men.

"What? I haven't heard anything new this morning. Well, at least not from the police."

He squints quizzically at me, and I shake my head. "Never mind. What did they find out?"

"Wasn't new information." He stands up, bags in hand. His mouth twists into a frown, and he grinds his teeth a bit before letting out a long breath. "She finally confessed. Martha Morrison confessed to killing my mother."

32

"He had to have found the money, don't you think?" Eden says, lounging in our cool, very cool, living room. She's wearing pajama pants and a T-shirt. I'm bundled up in sweatpants and a sweatshirt. Aiden says we're crazy and that it's still hot in the house. Of course, Eden is cuddled up against him on one of the couches, so maybe that's what has him too warm.

"Really? He seemed sincere," I say as I reach for my cup of decaf. "I don't know."

Timothy left after we talked. I left messages for anyone I thought might know about Martha Morrison's confession, but I got automatic 'out of office' replies from both Charlie and Lucy. No one else I talked to knew much. I did talk to Victor but only about the air conditioning in a short, curt conversation that took place at the rear of his truck as he loaded up. He said he'd covered the details with Craig on the phone, and honestly, I'm good with that. He acted sad, but I wonder if he's just not ready to accept what his wife has done.

Eden is very glad our houseguest is gone. She still swears he was creepy, but I think she's just battling how attracted she was to him on the night of the tequila shots. I think it scared her, and that's a good thing. It's never good to assume you're bulletproof enough to put yourself in the way of temptation. Especially when tequila is involved.

"Of course he found the money," Eden presses on. "How else can he be so blasé about moving away before he has the money from the sale of the house?" She wrinkles her nose. "I mean, I thought he was broke."

Aiden kisses her on top of her head. "You could be right. Mrs. Morrison has always said she knows nothing about the money."

"Aiden!" I scold him. "You said you didn't know anything about Mrs. Morrison's confession. We didn't know she said that about the money!"

"Well, I don't know much. She just broke

down and said she did it. That's about it. I
mean, what more do you want her to say?"

"I don't know," I grumble. "Where is your
mother?" I get up from my lounge. "She said
she'd take the rest of the desserts out of here.
Anyone else want anything?"

"Everybody at the station enjoyed them.
I sure hope Mrs. Church taught her daughter to bake this well!" He finishes with an
"oomph," and I figure Mrs. Church's daughter showed him what she thinks of that.

"Yoo-hoo! Anybody home in this refrigerator?" Annie pushes in the front door.

"Come into the kitchen," I greet her.
"You've got to have a piece of baklava. Want
a cup of decaf?"

"Sure thing. Hey there, you two," she
greets her son and his girlfriend. "Aiden,
don't look so comfortable. No need for you
to stay here tonight now that author-boy is
gone. Besides, you need to come home. It's
garbage night." She sails on into the kitchen.
"Feel that air conditioning! Welcome to the
twentieth century! Or is it the twenty-first?
I never remember." She's wearing a short,
green cotton dress with white seashells printed all over it. "I love Kerry's baklava." Picking
out her piece she leans toward me and whis-

pers, "Sure is a good thing for us that that woman gets emotional at the drop of a hat!"

"So, this isn't unusual?" I whisper back.

"Well, this is a bit over the top quantity-wise. She must've been real upset."

Noise from the coffee maker covers us a little, so I stand up instead of talking over the box of goodies. "She was. I was too. The whole thing has been upsetting but has opened my eyes."

Annie shakes her head and widens her eyes. She didn't hear it from me, but she knows all about Victor being abused by Martha. Apparently everyone does. All I know is I didn't tell anyone.

I hand her a plate. "Here, put some on this to take into the living room. The rest of the box is for you to take wherever you're taking it."

"To the church. The youth group is doing a beach day tomorrow, so they'll devour these." She takes a bite, then mumbles, "I might keep the baklava, though."

Chuckling at her, I carry the plate and some napkins into the living room, breaking up a make-out session in the process. "Eden thinks Timothy found the money," I say to give the young people a minute to pull apart.

"Sounds about right to me. Although, if

the festival folks ever find out he has it, he better be looking over both shoulders!" Annie laughs and plops down on the other end of the couch. Eden sits up a bit straighter. There's nothing like sitting next to your boyfriend's mother to quench passion's fire.

I look at my phone when I sit down. "I can't understand Lucy not answering my messages. Wonder if her phone is on the fritz. She's always on it."

Aiden rests his elbows on his knees. "Maybe she's with her momma. Miss Birdie was pretty upset about Mrs. Morrison's confession. She came down to the station and everything."

Eden smacks him on the arm, and I say, "Thank you, Eden." Then I demand of Officer Bryant, "Why didn't you tell us that earlier?"

His girl scoots closer to his mother but shakes a finger at him. "How many times do we gotta ask you what's going on? What's Miss Birdie upset about?"

He shrugs, but as he does he leans away from Eden's hitting arm. "Don't rightly know. She and some other women from their Sunday school class were down there raising Cain."

Annie says, even with her mouth full, "Hit him again."

Eden complies. "So there was more than just Miss Birdie. Was Miss Lucy there?"

Aiden jumps up, out of arm's reach. "No. I mean, I don't think so." My phone rings, and he looks at it like it's the governor calling with his stay of execution.

"Charlie!" I answer. "Hi. I've been trying to reach you."

"Am I on speaker?"

I look around. Annie is shaking her head no, Eden is grimacing, and Aiden is holding his arm and looking at the floor like a sad puppy.

"Yes. But it's just me, Aiden, Eden, and, uh, Annie."

"Okay. Have you or Annie talked to Lucy this afternoon?"

Annie shouts, "No," and I say, "Me neither. She hasn't called me back. Or even texted."

He grunts. "Great. Miss Birdie is driving me crazy. Finally got her to go home. Can you go over and sit with her until Lucy shows up?"

"Sure. Is she okay?"

"As far as I can tell. Just madder than a wet hen. Lucy usually can calm her down,

but I don't know where she's gotten off to.
I've got to go."

"Okay, we'll check in on Miss Birdie.
Bye."

Annie and I get up, leaving only Eden
seated. We carry in the plate of baked goods
and add them to the box in the kitchen. I
find some flip-flops and finish my last sip of
coffee. Annie takes another sip of hers and
then pours it down the drain as she asks,
"You want to ride with me?"

"You'd have to bring me all the way back
here."

"No problem. It's not that far out of my
way."

We are both halfway out the front door
when Annie leans back in. "Aiden?"

He turns from where he was just getting
ready to settle back in beside Eden on the
couch. "Yes, Momma?"

"Garbage. Don't sit back down. Go
home."

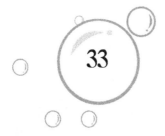

33

"She wouldn't even take me down to the police station. What kind of a daughter is that? You tell me." Miss Birdie veers from mad to sad without ever leaving her cushioned rocking chair. Her rocking pace doesn't miss a beat. Annie tried resting her arm on it to maybe slow the older woman down, but Miss Birdie shoved her arm off and glared at her. Annie won't be doing that again.

I'm sitting forward on the edge of the couch, leaning close to the fast-moving chair—not too close, of course. "I know she had a very busy day at work today. Did she maybe have a meeting tonight? A council meeting or something? Maybe something at church?"

I look around the room. Along with An-

nie and me, there are five other women, and
a couple of them look as old as Miss Birdie.
One is sound asleep in a chair near the sliding doors of Miss Birdie's beach house. One
is in the kitchen muttering to herself. I think
she said she's putting together a breakfast casserole. For whom she didn't seem quite sure.
I think she's one of those people who can't sit
still when they're worried. The woman next
to me is praying under her breath, just loud
enough to be a buzz in my ear. The other two
women are in chairs they've pulled up to face
Birdie. Annie and I are trying to get the full
story from them. It's not working so far.

"Why won't Charlie listen to us?" one of
the women asks in her gruff, country voice.
"Annie, he knows we wouldn't just make stuff
up. Martha did not kill that woman. Seems
we've earned the right to be listened to and
believed by now!"

Annie lets out a big sigh. "But Miss Dot,
she admitted to it. She says she put that stuff
in the muffins and then gave them to her.
She knew what she was doing."

Dot, a tall, skinny woman with deeply
tanned skin and bright, white hair, huffs at
Annie, then reaches out to stop Birdie's chair
cold. "Birdie! Enough of this. We have to
let them know everything. You know what I

mean. If this woman"—here I get a shake of her head in my direction—"if she has Charlie Greyson's ear, then we've got to tell it all."

The woman seated next to Annie moans and rubs her hands together. "I've shared with the class too much for us to become blabbermouths now. What happens in Sunday school is sacred to me. How can it not be for all of you? No, absolutely not! How do I know you won't start shooting your mouths off if I get in trouble?" She's wearing a turquoise sweater set and black slacks. Her jewelry looks expensive, and so does her hairstyle. While Dot looks like she just stepped out of her garden, this lady in turquoise looks like she just stepped out of an ad for a ritzy senior living center. The other women are somewhere in the middle.

The woman in the kitchen bangs down a pan. "For the love of Pete! Louise, if you ever get threatened with jail for lying about coloring your hair and getting Botox, then don't worry one second. We'll let 'em hang you from the highest tree before we spill! Dot, tell them what they need to know to help Martha. I gotta get home. It's already full dark out there."

Dot smirks a bit at her fancy friend, but reaches out and clasps one of her manicured hands. One hand has nails with bright pink polish while the other is caked with dirt, but they hold on tightly. Dot closes her eyes before saying, "We think Martha's been brainwashed."

Annie and I both deflate. We thought we were getting somewhere. I ask, "Why do you think that?"

"Because she's not been herself and she would never kill someone. Y'all don't know what all we know. You just have to trust us," Dot explains.

Birdie sets to rocking again. "See? They think we're crazy. I told you not to say it. I told you all. They want proof."

"Did you tell this to Lucy?" Annie asks.

Birdie rolls her eyes at us. "Duh. That's what set her off wailing about that poor man. 'That poor, poor man!' My daughter is a sucker for a sob story. She's probably off with Davis right now complaining about how she has to live her with her old mother and how her mother is crazy. She probably thinks I'm going to kill her like she thinks Martha poisoned that woman. Although it'd have to be some other way since I don't cook no more!" Birdie stops her rocking and pushes to stand up. "I'm going to get in bed and watch TV in my room. Tell my daughter not to wake me when she comes in!"

We are all dumbstruck as we watch the tiny woman march to her room and slam the door as much as she is capable of slamming it.

I look around the room. "She doesn't really think all that about Lucy, does she?"

Dot shrugs, but Louise smiles her magazine advertisement smile. "Oh no, darling. She's just overwrought." She stands. "We probably all are. What we need is a good night's sleep. Somebody wake Nancy up and tell her it's time to drive us home."

Annie jumps up. "How about I drive everyone home?" She looks at me, and I nod in encouragement. "Jewel will stay here with Birdie, and y'all can figure out cars tomorrow, okay?"

The lady comes out of the kitchen, turning the light out behind her. "Sounds good to me. Come on, ladies. Stan's going to think they locked me up with Martha."

Without Birdie the gang seems to have lost its fire. They troop out onto the deck walkway and then down the stairs—slowly. Annie is following them, so I step out onto the deck. She looks back at me. "You're good here?"

"Oh sure. I'll keep trying to track down Lucy. Do you think it's like Birdie said, that she's just mad and off sulking?"

"Possibly. You know how in the good old days before cell phones you could just disappear for a few hours and get your head together? Lucy does have a lot on her plate. Maybe she just turned off her phone and is somewhere having a drink or just driving around." She looks down the stairs. "I better go. Coming, ladies!"

Walking back into the living room I hear my name being called. I hurry to Birdie's door and open it. "Are you okay?"

Only the bedside light illuminates the room. Birdie is leaning up on her elbow, and when she sees me she waves me closer. "Jewel, honey, thank you. You didn't have to come, but I'm glad you're here. I heard Annie saying she's driving everyone home, so you tell her I appreciate that." She lays her head back on her pillow. "This all sure is a mess."

I take a couple more steps toward the bed. "I'm sure it's awful to see your friend in so much trouble. I remember when Craig was being accused of murder. It was just, well, awful."

Birdie stares up at the ceiling and sighs. "But that was just a mistake. I can't help but feel this is plain ol' evil. Evil Martha can't even see any longer. Y'all just don't understand. You're strong, young women who..." She flops over on her side, looking away from me.

I wait for a minute to see if she'll continue. Evil? Of course premeditated murder is always evil, but she acts like there's more to it than that. "Miss Birdie, is there anything I can do for you? To help you ladies get through this?"

She sighs again, then rolls toward me. "Pray I can get these ladies to open up and let me prove what we think is going on."

I can feel my eyes widen, unblinking. "Prove it? You have proof? Miss Birdie, the police need any proof that you have."

She rolls back and settles into her covers. "Can you turn my light out? I forgot to before I turned over, and now I'm comfortable. Good night, Jewel."

She seems to already be asleep by the time I turn off the light. She could be faking it, but either way she's done talking. I leave the room, pulling her door almost shut.

What kind of proof could she have? And why hasn't she taken it to the police?

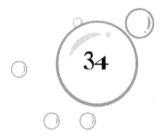

34

"Is Mother asleep?"

"Lucy?"

My friend holds her finger to her mouth as she slips in the sliding glass doors. She tiptoes to her mother's room and steps inside. After only a couple of minutes, she's coming back through the door and pulling it closed.

"She's asleep. Thank goodness. I could not take one more rant about Martha Morrison."

I stand as she rushes toward me and envelops me in a hug. "Oh, you are just a doll to stay here with her." She pulls me into the kitchen with her. "Wine? No. I think just water. But do you want wine?"

"No, thanks. Where have you been?"

She sighs at me and rolls her eyes. Getting

a glass and filling it from a filter jug in the refrigerator, she offers it to me. Then she fills one for herself. She's still in her work clothes, a white, silky top under a purple jacket with three-quarter-length sleeves. Her skirt is the same deep purple with white stripes at the bottom. It's hard to imagine purple being business wear, but on Lucy it's very polished, sedate even. Her hair, however, looks like it's been through the ringer. Even as I'm watching her, she runs her hands through it. Weariness shows in the droop not only of her shoulders but in the lines on her face. She looks exhausted, and I'm not sure I've ever seen her like this.

"Come sit down. Drink your water," I say as I pull her toward the living room.

She pauses, looking out the sliding doors toward the beach. "I was thinking of sitting out there, but it's still hot. It feels so good in here." She turns. "I've never been as happy as I was when I got your last text saying the Sunday school ladies were gone and Mother was in her bedroom." She eases onto the couch. I'd put the chairs the ladies had moved around back and straightened up the room while I was waiting for her.

"You could've answered one of my thousand texts so we weren't so worried."

She reaches out to pat my knee. "I know. I apologize, but I was in meetings all day down in Jacksonville. Even muted my phone. Then when I did look I was drowning in texts and calls from the Sunday school gang, the police station, my friends, and Davis, whose daughter was in a car accident in Kentucky. She's fine, broke her leg, but he flew out there today." She stretches and yawns. "And poor Victor. I don't know if he'll make it through all this with Martha." She expels a breath in frustration. "And my mother and her posse sure aren't helping!"

"You've talked to him?"

She cocks her head. "I think I hear Annie outside, but yes, we arranged to meet so that he could hand over the Shrimp Festival files to me. No way could I talk to Victor as rattled as he is, get all the details, and pay attention to my phone all at the same time. The Shrimp Festival is a year-round endeavor, and he doesn't need more on his plate right now, so he turned it all over. I have a trunk full of files and notebooks. Hopefully Martha's confession means there won't be a trial, but he says he has to concentrate all his energy on helping her. I find it hard to believe he is planning on sticking beside her," she hisses as we turn to see Annie coming in the doors.

"All safely delivered!" she says loudly until we both shush her. "Oh, Birdie's asleep? Good." She leans over to hug Lucy. "We've been worried about you, girl!"

"I was just explaining how crazy everything has been," Lucy says. "Y'all were so wonderful to look out for Mother and her friends; they can be a handful." She smiles at me. "You didn't know Birdie Fellows when she was in her heyday. She could run rings around me!"

"I find that hard to believe," I say, but Annie backs her up.

She stretches her eyes wide and opens her arms. "You saw a bit of it tonight. She about rocked that chair through the floor. She was some kind of riled up." Annie laughs. "Lucy, you should've heard Greyson when he called. He was at his wits' end!" We laugh and then quiet ourselves.

I lean forward. "Lucy, your mother said something about having proof about what she and her friends were saying."

Annie scrunches her face. "She didn't say anything about any proof when I was here. What's she talking about?"

I nod. "It was after you left. She mentioned it and then asked me to turn off the light and went to sleep. Any idea what she was talking about?" I ask Lucy.

Once again she plows her fingers through her hair. "She's mentioned proof to me a couple times, but like you said, she immediately shut up about it when I wanted to know what it was. I'm afraid it's nothing, just a way to keep from giving up hope. The more I hear, the more I fear Martha Morrison is a truly troubled soul, but her friends just can't face that."

We almost sigh in unison; then we sit for a moment in the quiet, only the muted crashing of waves in the background.

Lucy stands. "Tomorrow is another day. Hopefully they'll realize Martha wouldn't confess unless she did it. Who would've believed everything else we've discovered about her and poor Victor?"

"He always seemed so in control and strong," Annie says with a sigh, "but I guess that just goes to show that you never know what goes on behind closed doors. You know, I never really was that fond of Martha. Of course I'd never tell that to your momma, but Martha always seemed pretty judgmental."

I slide open the door, and we step out onto the deck. It's dark, but there's enough light to see the white of the waves as they crest. "That's what Kerry Church says too."

Lucy goes to stand at the railing and look out at the ocean while Annie and I head to the stairs. She calls to us. "See you at lunch tomorrow, right? I guess there's no need to meet early to discuss the case, is there?"

That stops us, and we look at each other. Annie says, "I guess not, but it does help with parking, so I'll probably be there a bit early."

Lucy waves. "Well, don't wait on me. I'll be there by noon but not much before. Tomorrow is busy but hopefully not as crazy as today. Y'all want to help me unload my trunk?"

With all three of us it only takes one trip, and we leave Lucy surrounded by bags and boxes, sipping on a full-strength coffee.

Annie and I are quiet on the drive. There are few cars out, especially as we get farther away from the beach. Annie speaks as we pass over the marsh near the state park. "I loved Alan, but I can't imagine ever being so jealous I'd kill someone over him."

"I was thinking the same thing. I guess I'm not really the jealous type."

Annie doesn't say anything, but when I look at her I can see, in the lights from the dash, her mouth twisting from side to side.

"What?" I ask. "What are you thinking?"

"That you being a tad more jealous might not be a bad thing." She keeps her eyes on the road. "You and that husband of yours are just a little too detached. I mean, if you want to be detached, then go ahead and get divorced. But if you want to have a chance at saving your marriage, you're both going to have to start caring a bit more about what the other is doing."

"But... but he's not even here." I also stare straight ahead as we turn onto my street.

Neither of us says anything else until she pulls into the driveway. She puts the car in park and draws in a deep breath. "All I know is things aren't getting better like this." She looks at me, eyes focused. "And I'm not saying you want things to get better. I just know if it were me and Alan and our kids and grandkids, I hope I'd try a little harder before letting it all go."

My lips feel glued together, though not to keep any words inside. There are no words trying to work themselves out. There's no anger or hurt or—anything. I open my door, and she reaches out to me.

"Jewel, honey, don't be mad."

I look out at the dark and then back at her. My lips part, and I smile. "I'm not mad."

Then I sigh. "But, well, you're right." I get out of the car, close the door, and walk up the front steps. I push the door, the unstuck door, into heaven.

Cool, air-conditioned heaven.

After Annie's words I might have trouble sleeping, but it won't be because I'm sweating or that I'm worried I have a murderer living downstairs.

All in all, it's been a good day.

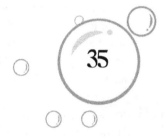

35

Sleep was a long time coming and filled with awful dreams when it did. Poisoned muffins. Craig on a sailboat with Martha Morrison, then with Lucy. My kids all there with them. I was in our house, or no, it was supposed to be this house, but it was much creepier, and Timothy was the owner. Or Eden. Or her mother. Kerry was some kind of witch, and she was putting poison into everything she baked, and I couldn't stop eating it.

At dawn I got up and went downstairs. The blessedly cool downstairs. I ate a banana while I wandered around. No workers. No Timothy. Just Eden, who would be leaving for work before long. I went back upstairs, lay down, and fell sound asleep.

Sleeping in a bit, not until almost noon

like Kerry Church, since I moved here has been a double-edged sword. First, it means no alarm, so that's a good thing. However, waking up tangled in sweaty sheets is not a good way to start the day. Today I fully enjoyed waltzing down the stairs a bit later than usual, and even after a long night, I feel refreshed. And alone. Yes, this is going to be a good day.

As soon as I press start on my cup of coffee, I dial Craig. Annie was right last night. I don't know where this is going, but I've got to start caring.

"Jewel. Hey," he answers.

"Good morning! I'm calling from a very cool house. The air is working perfectly!"

"Good to hear, since Victor was such a pain about getting the money wired. Why he couldn't just have you write him a check is beyond me."

"Well, he's had a bunch of crazy stuff going on here. His wife confessed to that murder. Um, did I tell you about that?"

"I knew she was in jail. You know, I think I met her one time."

"Really? You met Martha Morrison?"

"Yeah. Right after we moved in. He came around one day while I was out in the yard. She was with him, and he introduced us. He wanted to drop off his card. So, you're saying she murdered someone?"

"A woman she thought Victor was seeing. Jealousy, I guess."

He laughs. "That's hard to believe. She doesn't seem the type to be jealous of anyone."

"Why do you say that? Martha Morrison is like most of us women. Getting older and less confident." I think about what Annie said. "Like when I heard you were going sailing with friends down there, I might've gotten a little jealous." I sink onto a kitchen chair.

"Uh, well, there's no need for that. It was work people. And you don't look old. Morrison's wife isn't old either; I guess that's what I was thinking. But what do I know? Listen, I better get back to work."

There's a pause. I've said enough for today. "Okay. Have a good one, and we'll talk later. Thanks again for handling everything with the air."

We hang up, and I'm angry that my knees feel quivery as I walk over to get my cup of coffee. How in the world will we ever fix anything if one little phone chat makes me a wreck?

Colby's Seafood sits on old pilings in the middle of Sophia Beach Marina. Apparently it was originally a welcome center. Now it's a favorite spot for tourists and locals to eat, inside or out on the wide, painted porch, watching the sunset and the life of the marina—fishing boats with their chartered guests, tour boats taking families up the river to Cumberland Island, private boats strung with party lights, and even the occasional luxury yacht.

This isn't an old-fashioned seafood place; Colby's is more of a fine dining restaurant with soothing music, not beach reggae. Carpets, not worn planks. Wine glasses, not plastic cups. I love living in a town that offers both. Tamela and Cherry are seated at a long table near the side windows looking out over the water. Floating docks surround the restaurant's big porch, and the wide-open St. Mary's River flowing to the Atlantic Ocean is just beyond them.

Annie and I ran into each other in the parking lot, so we walk in together.

"The lot is getting full. I'm glad we got here early," Annie says.

"We wondered if you'd show up early

since there wasn't anything to talk about," Cherry says. "We decided to come on down and get our table. But now that we're here, anything new?"

Tamela leans forward. "I heard Miss Birdie was causing a ruckus at the police station yesterday. How is she? Have you talked to Lucy?"

Annie rolls her eyes. "Birdie was still a mess last night. I haven't heard from Lucy today. She said she'll be here but closer to noon."

"Poor Miss Birdie," Tamela says, shaking her head.

"Can I get you ladies some water?" the waiter asks, and I do a double take. He's one of the young men that has been working on our air conditioning.

"Hector! I didn't know you worked here too."

He looks a little uncomfortable before answering. "Not 'too,' Mrs. Mantelle. Your house was the last one. Mr. Morrison is out of business."

"I didn't realize that."

The others shaking their heads and frowning at me tells me no one else knew either.

He shrugs. "It happens. I don't make as much here, but it's a whole lot cooler!" He grins at us. "Let me know if you need anything. I'll get your orders once everyone arrives, all right?"

Annie frowns. "I guess poor Victor just had more than he could stand."

"I guess, but I have trouble believing he just closed up like that," I say.

"Well, you're really not going to believe this," Tamela says, pulling a piece of paper out of her purse. "Timothy Raines is in seventh heaven!"

"Why?" I scoff. "Did he already sell his mother's house?"

"No, silly." Tamela waves the printout in front of my face. "This. He's sold rights for his books to a movie company."

"What?" I take the article and skim it. "Oh my goodness. That's a lot of money. I bet he is happy." I hand the paper to Annie. "I guess Eden was wrong. Maybe he didn't find the money his mom stole from the Shrimp Festival."

My phone rings, and I sneak a peek at it, finding myself relieved it isn't Craig. All morning I've been afraid he would call me back. I'm such a chicken. "It's Charlie," I tell the others. "Hello?"

"Morning. Listen, uh, we're going to have to let Martha Morrison go."

"What!"

Everyone stares back at me, confused and questioning.

"I can't believe I'm saying this," Charlie continues, "but Miss Birdie and her friends brought in their Sunday school prayer journal this morning."

"Prayer journal!" I blurt. "I bet that's the proof she was talking about."

Charlie growls, "Why they didn't bring this in from the start is beyond me. Although some of the ladies even today didn't want Birdie to let me read it. One was moaning about it being sacred." He lowers his voice. "They really aren't going to like it when they find out I have to keep it for evidence. It's full of Martha's history, including the name of the therapist she has been seeing for years. The long and the short of it: there's no way she killed Amanda Raines."

"Really? Have you talked to the therapist? What did he say?"

"She. The therapist is a woman who, you're not going to believe this, specializes in reversing brainwashing. Especially for cults, but she works more with spouses who do it. She talked to Mrs. Morrison on the phone and helped her talk to us. It's filled in a lot of blanks."

"Hold on." I stand up and motion for the women to come with me, saying, "You have to hear this, but we need to go outside." We move away from the table, and I speak into the phone. "I'm putting you on speaker. It's just us—you know, *us*. Well, except Lucy's not here yet."

We push out onto the side porch and huddle in a corner where there's no one around. "Okay, so, you're saying Victor has been brainwashing Martha?" Everyone's eyes and mouths pop open.

"Apparently. There's a lot more. We're looking for Victor and wanted to tell you ladies to keep your eyes open and, well... where are you?"

"Colby's."

"Oh. Oh yeah, your Wednesday lunch. I just don't want to send Miss Birdie home alone. The other ladies left, but she won't leave until Martha is released, and that takes a while. I kind of have my hands full, and just like yesterday I can't find Lucy."

Annie says, "She should be here any minute. Don't you worry about Miss Birdie. You tell her to sit tight. One of us will be right there to get her. Maybe I'll bring her down here to have lunch with us."

"Thanks. Can't believe I let the others get

out of here without her, but it was kind of crazy."

Cherry moves closer to the phone. "So, you think Victor did it? Killed Amanda?"

He hesitates, and we wait. Finally he says, "Victor did something. We're just not sure what."

I jump in. "Did you know he closed his company? Our house was the last one he worked on. Oh, and Craig said this morning he wouldn't take a personal check. The payment had to be wired."

"No, we didn't know that, but that settles it. I'm putting out an APB. Appreciate y'all taking care of Birdie." He hangs up, and we are all left staring at each other.

"Everything all right?" One of the ladies in our lunch group has come to the side door. "We could see y'all out here and thought we'd better check."

We look inside to see others have shown up and are looking at us, smiling and waving.

"We'll be right in," Annie yells. As we begin walking she says, "I'll go get Miss Birdie and see if she wants to have lunch with us. I'll call and let you know."

At the table, Annie collects her purse and phone while the rest of us take our seats. We're rattled, but there's nothing more for us to do. I lay my phone down so that I can see if I get a call or text and wonder out loud, "I'm surprised Lucy isn't here yet."

One of the women seated across the table and down from me says, "Lucy must've changed plans. She won't be here for lunch."

"What? Why do you say that?" I ask.

"I had to park in the next parking lot, way down there." She points to a gravel overflow lot at the end of the marina. "Lucy was getting on a boat near those docks there. I hollered at her, but she didn't hear me." She raises her eyebrows and chuckles. "And her friend she was cuddled up to did *not* look like Davis Reynolds. Wonder who she's going on her lunch sail with?"

Annie is still standing between our table and the doorway. "She was with a man?" Her voice is squeaky, and my stomach begins to sink.

"What did he look like?" I ask.

"Big-shouldered and with a headful of dark-black hair." Our friend has picked up on our nerves, and her voice softens. "Why?"

I grab my phone and go to my recent calls. "You remember anything about the boat?" I ask as I push to connect with Charlie.

"Sure." She turns and looks out the windows. "There. That one."

It's a large sailboat. And it's underway, headed for the ocean.

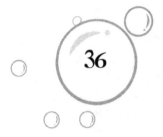

36

Again we rush from the table. This time, though, we're accompanied by another half-dozen women. One with a walker. We go out the side door and down the ramp to the main dock. The sailboat looks so peaceful. I'm filling Charlie in on what we've learned, and he's yelling everything to someone on his end.

"It's going to be past the docks soon!" I yell. "Hurry!"

"I'm headed there. We've got it covered."

We watch until the boat is almost out of sight, and then we realize how hot it is in the full sun on the dock and move back inside. Annie's son Adam, one of the marina managers, meets us there.

"Momma! What's going on? Harbor pa-

313

trol and police are swarming all over. Coast
Guard too." He hugs her. "I shouldn't have
been surprised that you knew more than us
in the office. Your text was the first notice
we got."

She pulls away from his hug and looks
him in the eye. "Victor Morrison is trying to
escape, and he's got Lucy on that boat!"

Adam shakes his head. "That boat isn't
registered to Victor Morrison."

Charlie comes hurrying up. "No, it isn't.
He's changed his identity. Somehow Lucy is
involved."

Annie exclaims, "Charlie Greyson, you
know she isn't involved with that man in any
way, shape, or form!"

He stares at us. "Either she's involved or
she's a hostage. Take your pick."

Annie gasps. "That's a stupid pick. Just
get her back."

The restaurant has closed off the room we
are in, and the police have taken over a table. The other ladies in our lunch group have
been given a table out in the general area,
and we are giving them updates. Except we
don't know much more than they do already.

The Coast Guard and police are supposed
to stop the boat and apprehend Victor. Char-

lie and the other officers say this calmly, but I see the worry on their faces.

Hector slides in the door. "Miss Jewel? You wanted to see me?" His eyes bounce from me to Officer Greyson, who is bearing down on him.

"You Hector Greenway?" Charlie asks. "You worked for Morrison?"

"Yes, sir." He looks at me as I step to his side. Then he nods. "I told Miss Jewel he's closed now."

"Why would he do that?" Charlie demands.

Hector shrugs. "Retired. Gonna sail, he said. I mean, you know about his wife killing that woman?"

Then something Craig said this morning comes to me, and I step closer to the young man. "Hector, was Mr. Morrison ever around you with other women? Women who were not his wife?"

The room goes quiet. Hector's eyes flare, and he takes a step back.

I step into the void he left. "Please. It's important."

He frowns at me, then looks sad. "Sometimes. I'm not saying he was a good man, or husband, but he was good to work for because he had to pay a lot."

Charlie looks confused. "Why did he have to pay a lot?"

Hector shrugs again, and then a resigned look crosses his face. With a sigh he explains. "His temper, but hey, he's the boss, and I was good with that. Other guys, not so much. Mr. Morrison wants things done his way? I can do that."

Annie has meandered to my side, and she says in my ear, "Doesn't sound like an abused husband, does it?"

I grunt and turn to look out the windows in the direction the sailboat went. "No. It also doesn't sound like someone Lucy should be alone on a boat with."

"Sir?" A uniformed officer rushes over to Charlie. "We found this near where the boat was docked."

Charlie reaches for the evidence bag, and a groan escapes from Tamela. In the clear plastic bag is Lucy's phone in its distinctive, hot-pink case. It's been smashed.

The officer explains. "We found it in the weeds to the side of the marina office, near where the lady said she saw Ms. Fellows and Mr. Morrison getting onto the boat."

Tamela groans again and weakly says, "That looks like she didn't go willingly." My stomach does another flop as I watch the of-

ficers' looks of concern. Charlie's eyes meet
mine for just a moment before I turn to sit
down.

Then the radio crackles to life, and we all
swirl in that direction. There's shouting and
something that sounds like gunfire coming
through the speaker. I can't understand what
is being shouted outside of the orders to drop
a weapon. There's one scream that is most
definitely Lucy's. Annie grabs my hand.

Tension fills the room, and even though
I'm covered in sweat, I'm freezing. One of my
newest and closest friends is out in the middle of the ocean, vulnerable and in the line of
fire, and there's nothing I can do about it. My
whole body feels like overcooked noodles.
Annie stands beside me, gripping my hand.
There's some more shouting, then a pause,
which I can barely tolerate. Then, somehow,
mercifully, the shouting becomes calm, if au-
thoritative, talking. I recognize the cadence
of the Miranda warning. Suddenly, as one,
the officers take a deep breath and relax.

Charlie shifts toward our table, trans-
lating the codes and phrases being reported
over the walkie-talkie to dispatch. "It's over.
Lucy is fine. Victor is in custody."

Annie hugs me, practically lifting me

from my chair. Then Tamela grabs my arm a bit woozily. "Oh, I need to sit down."

"Here," I say, pushing the chair toward her. We all take deep breaths as our heart rates calm. The officers begin gathering their equipment.

Aiden sticks his head into the room. "I've got Miss Birdie here. She forced me to bring her. She wouldn't go home, even after I told her everything's over." He gets pushed from behind, and he moves to the side. He waves the little woman in, and we all jump up to greet Lucy's mother. However, her look of disdain quickly stills the room.

Chin high in the air, she looks around. "I'm happy my daughter is safe, but if she'd just listened to me from the beginning, all of this could've been avoided! Charlie, bring me a Singapore Sling."

Charlie nods at the waiter, who had followed them into the room, and then gives Miss Birdie an arm to help her to the table. As she's getting arranged Annie raises her eyebrows at me and whispers out of the side of her mouth, "Lucy might've been better off sailing away with Victor than living with her mother after this."

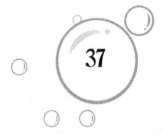

37

"There was a docking receipt in one of the Shrimp Fest folders Victor gave me last night. Something about it didn't look right, plus it didn't belong in the folders, so I thought since I was coming down here for lunch, I'd swing by the marina office and ask about it."

Lucy has a plate of fried shrimp in front of her, and now that she's eaten several she's ready to tell her story. We all ate while she was talking to the police and Coast Guard and everyone else who could crowd into that back room. We're at a smaller table next to the windows out front, where the marina has calmed down to its usual early summer pace. Even the seagulls are resting from their lunchtime frenzy over dropped French fries and unbussed tables.

Miss Birdie began to crash after all the excitement but not before she told us her part in seeing justice served; how she finally got through to the other Sunday school ladies that their prayer journal would help explain what they were trying to tell everyone—though I remember her saying exactly the opposite last night.

She and some of the ladies had thought for a while that Victor was playing games with his wife. The prayer requests for fixing her behaviors that were driving her husband crazy didn't match up with the Martha Morrison they knew. She wanted God to help her grandchildren like her and want to be with her, and she wanted the Peeping Tom neighbors who looked in her windows at night to move away. The only thing Victor didn't seem to convince her of was to stop going to church and talking to her Sunday school friends. But she wouldn't believe them, or the therapist she saw occasionally, that she wasn't the awful person her husband said she was.

As Victor mentally, and sometimes physically, abused her, he made her believe she was the one doing the abusing, and she lived in fear of the police coming to lock her up—a fear again fed by her manipulative husband. When the police did arrive to inquire into

Amanda's murder, Martha lost all ability to reason and, at her husband's suggestion, eventually confessed to killing Amanda.

Birdie's exhaustion, aided by her Singapore Sling, finally took over, and Annie called the pastor and his wife. As soon as Lucy arrived, and Miss Birdie got to hug her daughter, they took her home.

So it's me, Annie, Tamela, and Cherry watching Lucy eat and hearing her side of the story. "I parked on the other side of the office, and with the docking receipt in hand I started up the sidewalk. Then around the corner comes Victor." She stops and sighs. "Okay. I have to say what I was *still* thinking: Poor Victor. That's how I'd come to think of him. Poor, poor Victor." Tears swim in her eyes, and she pushes her plate away. "How could I have been so stupid?" Her mouth twists shut, and she shakes her head.

"Don't beat yourself up," Cherry says, laying her hand on Lucy's arm. "He had a lot of practice at lying and fooling people. I talked to another nurse just a while ago, and she remembered one time when Martha came in with a sprained wrist. Victor had them thinking she'd hurt it hitting him, even though neither Victor nor Martha said anything outright. My friend is so upset that, even as a professional who knew what to look for, she had no idea."

Lucy takes a deep breath, which comes out ragged. "He was nothing but charming last night and even this morning—right up until he saw that receipt. He actually grabbed it from my hand and demanded to know where I'd found it and why I was snooping around in his business!" She pulls both her hands into her lap, rubbing her wrist. "He grabbed my wrist and said since I was so interested we were going to take a ride on his boat. I didn't know what in the world was happening!"

Annie grunts. "His boat! More like Sophia Island's boat! Stealing money from the festival to buy a boat! I've never heard of such craziness. Adam says Victor made the reservation for the marina online, so no one saw him, and no one thought a thing about it. Apparently they've tracked the purchase to him all in one lump sum. Festival money. So, what made you suspicious about the docking receipt?"

"The name on the receipt. First, I knew from some of the other festival paperwork that Victor is his middle name and his first name is Edward. The boat was registered to Ed Morris, not Morrison, but the name of the boat was *The Victor*. I guess while I was sleeping it all clicked that something wasn't right. I was going to call him this morning, but then, well, I didn't. Lord knows I still didn't suspect Victor of anything, not poor, poor Victor! But something…" She sadly shakes her head at us. "Anyway, I just thought I'd bring the receipt to the office and chat with them. See what they had to say. I don't really know what I was thinking, but when I saw his face looking at the receipt and then he grabbed my wrist, well, I knew immediately that I had it all wrong. There was absolutely nothing to feel sorry for this man about!"

Tamela shudders. "They found your phone, you know."

"Yes. They took it for evidence. It was in the front of my pocketbook, sticking half out of the pocket, and he pulled it out, dropped it on the sidewalk, and stepped on it. Up until that moment I guess I was in shock, but then I yanked to pull away from him and shouted. But there was no one in that area to hear me, and with the boats and cars, it was pretty noisy. He jerked me close to him, shoved the receipt in his pocket, and then pulled a gun out of that same pocket." She takes a moment to get a sip of iced tea. "Next thing I knew, he was hustling me up the gangplank to the boats."

"That's when Carol saw you," I say. "Thank goodness she did."

Tears brim again. "I heard her call me. I started to yell, but he pulled me even closer and said, 'I killed Amanda to make this work, and I really liked her. Don't think I won't kill you.'"

"He admitted it!" Annie gasps.

Lucy nods. "That and more. He seduced her and helped her steal the money. Like you said, he used the money to buy that awful boat, and he—"

"Oh wow!" I interrupt. "Pirate Mac said Amanda talked about sailing away. She was going to sail away with Victor!"

Lucy nods again. "Apparently that's what she thought, but once he had enough money for the boat, he was through with her. However, he knew if he left her behind she'd tell everyone. And he needed to get rid of Martha without a costly divorce."

"He told you all of this?" Cherry asks. "Or did you figure it out?"

"I figured some of it out, but he was pretty proud of himself. He locked me in a closet when we got on the boat, but it had a little window at the top so I could talk to him.

Once I was on the boat and I knew we were underway, I figured it wouldn't hurt for me to keep up the 'poor, poor Victor' line." She smiles up at the waitress as the young woman takes away her half-empty plate. We wait for the waitress to leave, then Lucy continues. "Of course he's such a blowhard he ate it up. Bragged about his whole scheme, thinking I was under his spell!"

Tamela leans back. "How did you stay so calm?"

"Well…" Lucy smiles, and a touch of sparkle returns to her eyes. "Don't tell Mother, but some of it was that I was so mad that I hadn't listened to her and the Sunday school ladies. I just flat-out dismissed them. They all danced around Victor not being what he seemed. Mother knew, *knew* Martha wasn't guilty, but I just dismissed her as protecting her friend. It didn't take long in that closet to connect all the dots. Mother never used the words 'brainwashing' or 'gaslighting.' I guess that would've been too close to what their prayer journal said. She just kept telling me Victor was pulling all the strings. That some men can control women." With a big frown, she admits, "I was too busy feeling sorry for him to see anything else."

Cherry repeats, "Don't beat yourself up.

Remember what I said. He's been doing this a long time." She lowers her voice. "And don't let your mother and her friends off the hook so easily. They should've come forward with more details."

"Wait," I say. "I'm not sure I understand the term 'gaslighting.' Is it just a new word for brainwashing?"

Annie says with a laugh, "It's not a new term because I know it. It's from a movie, right?"

Lucy and Cherry nod.

Tamela shrugs at me. "I don't know it either."

Annie is scrolling through her phone. "It's an old movie where the husband keeps messing with the gaslights in the mansion where they live, but he says nothing's happening, so the wife decides she's going crazy. He's also doing other stuff, but the gaslighting term is from the lights going up or down. Here it is: '1944 film *Gaslight* starring Charles Boyer and Ingrid Bergman.'"

"Oh!" Lucy exclaims. "I didn't remember Ingrid Berman was in it. I haven't seen it in years."

Tamela types into her phone. "I want to remember that so we can watch it." She looks up at us. "Sounds just like what Victor was doing. Poor Martha."

"I guess he was doing the same kind of thing to Amanda?" I ask.

Lucy sips on her tea. "Yes. He bragged about how he got her to take the money. He told her it was some kind of internal audit, and so the money was going right back into the festival. He said he had her thinking he worked part-time for the FBI. He told her after this investigation he was retiring and sailing the world and taking her along. I think she was lying to herself some too." She arches an eyebrow. "Victor being an FBI agent sure got a laugh from the police, but it sounds right up Amanda's alley, now that we know about her and Mac the Pirate."

Cherry sniffs. "That's true. But back to how he got rid of Amanda. Did he make the muffins?"

"No." Lucy swallows and looks sick to her stomach. "He—oh, he was so proud of this—he told Martha he needed all those stimulants to be able to have sex with her because she was so old, so of course she made the muffins." Tears come again. "It was just awful how he talked. He was very clear about not needing anything to keep women happy. He said he got Amanda to eat them because

he told her he had made them special for her,
but it was just their secret. He was stringing
her along just like he was Martha. I find it
hard to believe, and he might've been lying
again, but he said Amanda's affair with Mac
was his idea so people wouldn't suspect them
of their affair or of taking the money." She
presses her lips closed. Then she says, "Honestly, I think he likes pulling women's strings.
Playing with them. It was pure evil what all
he said!"

We are all silent for a moment. It's sickening to think of all the lies and manipula-
tions. Sickening to think of how many times
in recent days I've said, "Poor, poor Victor,"
to myself.

Lucy stands. "I have to go home and
apologize to Mother. Again. Davis will be
home tomorrow, and I'm taking off work on
Friday. I'm going to make him take me somewhere fun."

"Good idea. You deserve it," Tamela says
as the rest of us stand.

I slide next to Lucy as we walk to the
door. "Want me to give you a ride home?"

She smiles. "Thanks, sweetie, but I'm really okay. I was locked in that closet for most
of the time, and I jammed it so he couldn't
get it open without a lot of work. Besides,

he thought I was on his side, so it wasn't too scary. I knew he wouldn't get away." She smooths down her plaid pants and straightens the collar on her yellow cotton blouse as we come out onto the dock. Water, boats, and the heat greet us. It's hard to imagine all that has happened since I walked in those doors earlier. We pause along the railing and steady ourselves by taking in the beauty around us.

Annie grabs Lucy and hugs her. "Well, sugar, if you're gonna get kidnapped at gunpoint, you might as well do it on a pretty day on a nice boat!"

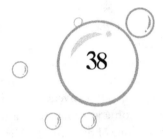

38

"I thought you were going away this weekend?" I say, leaning across the table to get a packet of Splenda for my coffee.

Lucy rolls her eyes at me. "You and me both. Davis needed it as much as I did with his daughter's car accident." She spreads her arms out. "Yet here we are."

'Here' is the fellowship hall at Lucy and Birdie's church on Saturday morning. The large room is filled with people, and everyone is here to say goodbye to Martha Morrison. She's seated at a table near the sunny windows, bracketed by her daughter and daughter-in-law. The men in her family stand behind her. They rallied around her and are taking her back up north to live with them the very minute this breakfast is over.

We move away from the coffee station and back to our seats. "All this was Mother's idea, but of course she got the younger Sunday school classes to do the work," Lucy says with a nod at the table near the front where Birdie and her classmates are as much the center of attention as Martha is.

"As they should!" Annie says, obviously eavesdropping on our conversation. "Lord knows I did my time washing about a thousand plates after one of these things. Hey, did y'all hear Amanda's house already has a contract on it?"

"Already? Did it even get on the market?" I ask. I left a message for Timothy, but he hasn't returned my call. Sounds like he's been busy.

"It didn't. That's got Amber's panties in a wad. She thought she had the inside track to get the listing, what with us solving Amanda's murder and all."

I pull out my chair and sit down. "I'm not sure we can take any credit for this one. Well, except for Lucy."

"Finding that docking receipt was just a fluke," Lucy says. Then she shrugs. "However, I've never been one to fail to take credit when someone wants to give it to me."

Annie leans over us both. "Kinda like

me and a margarita: if offered, I'm taking!"
She moves to her seat. "I hate that Cherry
couldn't make it this morning, but she said it
was a rough night at the hospital and she just
couldn't. Where's Tamela?"

"Over there with Hert." I motion for her
to come back to our table, as she looks bored.
"Hert found out Martha's son is a scuba div-
er, and he's thinking of taking it up. Here she
comes."

Tamela skirts through the tables and gets
to us just to throw her hands in the air. "That
man! I tried, but I give up. Martha's son is
stuck with him." She sits down. "I'm so full.
That casserole was delicious, and I must've
eaten my weight in strawberries. These will
be the last of the Florida ones, and I just
don't think the California ones are as good.
Did y'all hear about Tim's house?"

"Yep. Already sold," Annie says.

"Have you talked to him?" I ask.

"Hert has. Tim says he's ready to get out
of here, and I guess I can't blame him."

"I feel kind of bad," I admit. "I mean, I
actually suspected him of having something
to do with his mother dying. I'd like to con-
gratulate him and wish him well."

Lucy swats at me. "Don't worry one
bit. Him moving into your house and then

sneaking around. And lying on top of it all!"
She leans back to cross her legs and drink her
coffee as she gives me a shake of her head.
"What else *could* you think?"

With a look of gratitude I ask about her
mom. "Has Birdie calmed down at all?"

"She's honestly been pretty sweet. I think
once she had Martha out of jail, she relaxed.
Plus, I'm being very contrite." She leans forward suddenly. "There's Kerry Church."

We all shift to see the doors from the side
street closing behind the Churches. Kerry took the truth about Victor hard. Then,
when she realized she had helped put an innocent, troubled woman in jail, she took it
all even harder.

"She looks awful," Annie opines quietly,
and we all nod.

I whisper, "I've been trying to see her, but
Eden and Ted are the only ones she'll see or
talk to. Ted even closed the shop."

Annie sighs. "This can't be easy for her."

Lucy stands up. "No. I think I'll go walk
up there with her." She gets still, then asks,
"Y'all want to come?"

As we weave single file through the tables,
Kerry and Ted are walking up the side aisle,
so we reach the front corner at the same time.
Kerry's eyes widen when she sees Lucy, but

then they soften, and she opens her arms. She's wearing a plain, black dress that falls almost to her ankles. Her hair is dull and in a braid that looks several days old. Ted's hair is also ungroomed, and his tanned face is pale. Lucy goes to Kerry, and they hug. Then Kerry hugs each of us. When she gets to me, she hugs and releases me but holds me so that we can see each other.

"Eden is so fortunate to have you as a friend. I've loved having her with us, but she'll be back at your place today. Ted and I are taking a little healing trip."

"That's good to hear. You really have to forgive yourself. He was a manipulator and—"

"And he found a subject ready and willing to be manipulated when he found me." She looks at the floor, slowly shaking her head. "I'm supposed to be stronger than that." When she looks up, her face is tense. "And I will be stronger. Now, I need to go see Martha." We part, and she makes her way to the older woman who stands to greet her. They hold each other, and in just a moment they are crying. They aren't alone.

"I wanted to come with them," Eden explains later as she and I sit on the front porch, watching the sunset color the sky a vibrant orange, "but Mom said she needed me not to. She said she didn't want me watching and remembering her failure as a woman." Eden sighs. "Dramatic to the end."

"It was moving, and I'm sure it was hard, but I think it was necessary for her and Martha. They were both close to Amanda, so it was a time for them to grieve her too." I shift to lean against the railing on the front stairs. In just a few moments, the orange that colored our windows and led us outside has already faded. "I finally talked to Timothy, and he's not having a service for his mom here. Apparently there's a family burial plot somewhere in Indiana, and he's having her ashes taken there. It sounds like he is truly done with this town."

"Can't believe the house already sold." She stands up and stretches as she walks down the stairs to the old sidewalk, which is cracked and weedy. "I still think he was creepy, but I'm glad he's able to move on. I can't imagine burying my mom." Looking up at me she smirks. "Not that I'm not *sooo* glad to be back here."

"I completely understand." My voice trails off because, even as I understand, I

found out earlier today that my boys are going to spend a week with their dad in South
Florida and that they'll have no time to see
me. Understanding is not the same as accepting.

"Hey!" calls a man as he walks up our
palm-lined drive.

"Hey, Officer Greyson," Eden calls back.
"If you're looking for Aiden, he's not here.
His mom has him putting in some crepe
myrtles."

"Nope. Just out for a walk. Did you see
that sunset?" He ambles up to stand next to
Eden at the bottom stair.

I stay seated. "We saw the aftermath. Everything inside took on an orange glow, so
we came out to see the sky."

"It was magnificent over the marina," he
says as we watch Eden pull some weeds from
beside the sidewalk. For a little while there's
only the sound of her mild exertion, faint
sounds from Centre Street, and a few bugs
and frogs hurrying along the night.

Eden keeps working her way down the
sidewalk until she's halfway to the road. She
straightens up, looks back, and then points
away from us. "I'm going to take a walk
down to the marina." Before the sentence is
done she's striding even farther away, and it's

just the two of us on the porch. We watch her walk, and the silence lengthens with the shadows.

I take in a breath. "Charlie, I wanted to tell you thanks for talking to Timothy. I thought you were going to question him, maybe arrest him, but he said you were really helpful."

"I've found sometimes when a person dies, everyone around forgets their flaws. Especially if they were a basically good person, like Amanda. But the folks closest to them have trouble with all those warm, fuzzy memories. He needed to talk. He'll be fine. Besides, he's young." He says this as he raises his eyes to me and smiles.

"Yes. He is young," I agree with a laugh. "Still, it was exciting to have an author in the house."

Charlie walks up the first two steps, then leans against the railing below me. "I'm glad good things are happening for him."

"It's really good that he sold the house so quickly."

He nods. "I agree. It can be hard, but sometimes it's good to take the leap and move on." He leans away from the railing, stands straight, and plunges his hands into the pockets of his khaki shorts, but talks toward the porch floor. "The talk with Timothy was as good for me as it was for him. He was making his mother out to be a saint and prepared to spend his life punishing himself in her honor, despite what it would do to his life. As we talked I realized I was kind of doing the same." He lifts his head to look at me. "I left Fiona."

"Your wife?"

"Not for much longer. I saw a lawyer yesterday." He grimaces. "She's just not a nice person. Why I was punishing myself by staying with her, I can't fathom now. I mean, there are things in our past I regret, but…" He shrugs. "Anyway, I left." He looks to his right, where the sunset has long faded to gray. "I'm staying down at the Hampton Inn at the marina until the house closes. The Raines house is now the Greyson house."

"Timothy's—I mean, Amanda's house? You bought it? Isn't it just around the corner?"

"Yes." He stares at me and doesn't move a muscle. I swallow once, then again.

"We got air conditioning."

"That's what I hear."

I stand up. "Want something to drink? So you can see, well, feel the air conditioning?"

He chuckles. "Sure. I'd love to come feel your air conditioning."

Flustered, I turn quickly and scoot up the stairs, laughing. "You know what I mean!"

We step into the wonderful coolness. Charlie adds, "Oh, and congratulations."

He shuts the door, and I head to the kitchen. "On the air conditioning?" I lift a wine glass in question at him as he enters the room.

"Wine sounds great. No, congratulations on being the vice chair for next year's Shrimp Festival."

"Oh, no no no," I laugh as I grab a bottle of wine from the refrigerator. "I'm only Lucy's gofer. Just helping her out." I set the bottle next to the two glasses where he stands, and I look up at him.

He's grinning the proverbial ear-to-ear grin. "Oh really? And you say you've *met* Lucy Fellows?"

"But…" My mind swirls as he unscrews the wine and pours our glasses half full. I pick mine up. "Don't stop pouring there. I've got a feeling I'm going to need way more than that. And since I'm sure I can't get out of it—here's to the Shrimp Festival!"

Book 4 in the
Southern Beach Mysteries Series
is coming soon!

THE
SHARK
DID
IT

Check out all of Kay's Southern Fiction at
www.KayDewShostak.com
and she loves being friends on Facebook
with readers.

Here is the first chapter of book one in the Chancey series. Book nine in the series releases in 2021.

NEXT STOP, Chancey

CHAPTER 1

So how did I get stuck driving with my daughter, the princess, during one of her moods? Rap music, to pacify her, adds to my sense of disbelief. Carolina Jessup, you have lost your mind thinking this move can work.

Rolling hills of dry, green grass and swooping curves of blacktop lead us to a four-way stop. Across the road, sitting caddy-corner, is the sign I found so adorable last October. When we still owned a home in the Atlanta suburbs and moving hadn't entered the picture.

"Welcome to Chancey, Georgia. Holler if you need anything!"

A scream of "Help!" jumps to my lips, but that might disturb her highness. May-

be she's asleep and won't see her new home-
town's welcome.

"Holler? Who says 'holler'? Who puts it
on their sign for everyone to see?"

Nope, she saw it.

With a grimace, my voice rises above
Snoop Dog, or whoever is filling my car with
cringe-inducing music, as we cross the high-
way. "Honey, it's different from home, but
we'll get used to it, right? And Daddy's really
happy. Don't you think he's happy?" She dis-
misses my question, and me, by closing her
eyes and laying her head back.

I stick my tongue out at the sign as we
pass. I hate small towns.

Savannah sighs and plants her feet on the
dashboard, "All my friends back home want
me to stay with them on weekends." Drumming manicured fingernails on the door handle of my minivan she adds, "Nobody can
believe you did this to me."

Guilt causes my throat to tighten. "Honestly, Savannah, I'm having trouble believing
it, too." Apparently, she's tired of my apologizing because she leans forward and turns
up the radio. Rap music now pounds down
Chancey's main street, but no one turns an
evil eye on our small caravan. Two o'clock on
a Sunday afternoon, there's no one to notice

our arrival. July heat has driven everyone off the front porches, into air conditioned living rooms. Bikes and skateboards lie discarded in several yards, owners abandoning them for less strenuous activity, like fudgesicles and Uno.

Jackson is driving the rental truck ahead of my van in which our twenty years of life together are packed tighter than the traffic at home. Oh, yeah, Atlanta isn't home anymore. As the truck takes a curve, I have a view inside the cab. With their grins and high fives, they might as well be sitting on the driving seat of a Conestoga wagon headed into the Wild West. Next to Jackson in the truck is our thirteen-year-old, Bryan. Beside the passenger window is our older son, Will. Bryan is ecstatic about this move. Will just wants to get it done so he can get back to his apartment at the University of Georgia.

We slow to take a turn where two little boys in faded jeans lean against the stop sign post. After Jackson passes, the taller one steps toward the road and waves. I press the brake pedal harder and roll down the window. Humidity and the buzz of bugs from the weeds in the roadside ditch roll in.

"Hey guys."

"You moving here?" He punctuates his

question with a toss of his head toward the moving truck lumbering on down the road ahead of us.

"Sure are. I'm Carolina and this is Savannah."

The smaller boy twists the front of his red-clay-stained t-shirt in his hands and steps closer. "Ask 'em."

"I am," the speaker for the pair growls as he shoves his hand out to maintain his distance from the younger boy. "You moving up to the house by the bridge?"

"The train bridge?"

He nods and both boys' eyes grow larger. They lean toward me.

"Yes, you can come visit when we get settled."

Both boys shake their heads and the designated speaker drawls, "No, ma'am. Can't." He pulls a ball cap out of his back pocket and tips his head down to put it on.

The little one keeps shaking his head and finally asks, "Ain't you afraid?"

Savannah moans beside me, "Mom…"

"No, we like trains. Well, we'd better be going."

"You ain't afraid of the ghost?"

My foot jumps off the accelerator and

finds the brake pedal. My finger leaves off rolling up my window. "What?"

But they don't hear me. The boys are running toward the house sitting in the yard full of weeds.

Savannah grins for the first time today. "Did he say 'ghost'? Cool." She turns the music back up, lays her head against the headrest and we pull away from the corner.

Ghost? Like there's not enough to worry about.

Tiny yards of sunbaked grass and red dirt pass on the left. Across from them a string of small concrete buildings house a laundromat, a fabric store, and Jeans-R-Us. Chancey's version of an open-air shopping mall. Hopefully, Savannah's eyes are closed as I speed up to catch the truck. Over a small hill, the truck comes into view along with a railroad crossing. A smile pushes through my worries as I think of the grin surely on my husband's face right now.

For years, Jackson talked about moving and opening a bed & breakfast for railroad enthusiasts, railfans, in some little town. Now, a lot of people fantasize about living in a small town. I believe those are the people who have never lived in one—like my husband.

Only five weeks ago, he came home with a job offer from the railroad. We'd already experienced life with the railroad in our early married life. When we finally tired of his constant traveling, he took a job with an engineering consultant and we moved to the upscale suburbs northwest of Atlanta. Railroad job, or no, nothing was getting me out of the suburbs.

Then I find condoms in Savannah's purse, freak out, and accidentally make his dream come true. Well, the small town part of his dream, but the B&B is not happening. Things won't get out of hand again, not with me focusing.

At the railroad underpass there is no stop sign or light, but Jackson and the boys are stopped anyway. Arms poke out of both windows of the truck cab. There's no train coming but Bryan and Will spent more father-son outings in rail yards than parks so they could be pointing at one of a hundred things of interest.

At first Jackson's train obsession was cute, but I realize now, I'm an enabler. Like the husband walking down his basement stairs when it dawns on him his den could double as a scrap-booking store. Or the wife suddenly realizing her last ten vacations involved a NASCAR event.

Past the railroad yard and up the hill overlooking town, the harsh sunlight is muted by thick, leafy boughs drooped over the street. Shade allows for thick lawns encased behind wrought-iron fences or old-stone borders. Sidewalks cut through the lawns and lead to deep front porches and tall houses. The houses stand as a testament to Chancey's once high hopes—hopes centered on the railroad and the river. As we come to the top of the summit the River runs on our right. Savannah leans forward to look out her window, pushing her dark hair back. Ahh, even she can't ignore the view.

"Mom, you realize we are officially in the middle of nowhere, right? Look, nothing but trees and water as far as you can see. Not even a boat in all that water. I guess everybody's inside watching *The Antiques Roadshow*."

So much for enjoying the view. We turn away from the river and start back down the hill, taking a sharp turn to our right. A narrow road maneuvers through a green channel of head-high weeds. The road and weeds end in wide-open sky and a three-track crossing.

"Great, a stupid train already," Savannah growls. We can't see the train but up ahead her father and brothers are out of the truck and pointing down the line. We both know what that means.

I put the van into park and lay my head on the steering wheel. My sense of disbelief wars with the memory of the joy on my husband's face. Is it possible for us to be happy here? A train whistle blows as dark blue engines rock past and my head jerks up. Through the blur of rushing train cars I see the other side of the tracks—and our new home.

Frustration cuts through my sadness because someone is sitting on the front porch. Are you kidding me? A drop-in visitor already?

Find the rest of *Next Stop, Chancey* and the other Chancey books on Amazon.com or at your local bookstore.

CPSIA information can be obtained
at www.ICGtesting.com
Printed in the USA
BVHW072226240921
617234BV00001B/5

9 781735 099125